SHADOWS OF THE PAST

Longarm and his partner, Billy, were almost to the end of the barn. He was scouring a rickety freight wagon when he heard a strangled cry.

Whirling around, Longarm saw the silhouette of a man leaping up from under a rotting tarp and tackling Billy. He saw the man raise his arm and bring it down with a knife in his fist.

Longarm fired without thinking, and his bullet must have struck the attacker somewhere, because his shadow fell away from Billy and raced into the darkness.

"I'm stuck," Billy said, as he struggled to get up. "He stuck me pretty good, Custis."

"Just hang on, Billy," Longarm soothed. "Dr. Carter will get you fixed up."

"I hope so." Billy gazed up at his partner. "But if I don't make it, keep at it, Custis. don't let those murderers get away again!"

TABOR EVANS

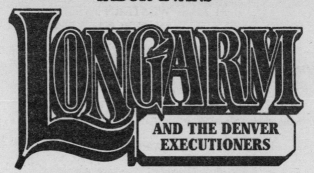

LONGARM

AND THE DENVER
EXECUTIONERS

JOVE BOOKS, NEW YORK

LONGARM AND THE DENVER EXECUTIONERS

A Jove Book / published by arrangement with
the author

PRINTING HISTORY
Jove edition / October 2001

All rights reserved.
Copyright © 2001 by Penguin Putnam Inc.
This book, or parts thereof, may not be reproduced in any form
without permission.
For information address: The Berkley Publishing Group,
a division of Penguin Putnam Inc.,
375 Hudson Street, New York, New York 10014.

Visit our website at
www.penguinputnam.com

ISBN: 0-515-13184-9

A JOVE BOOK®
Jove Books are published by The Berkley Publishing Group,
a division of Penguin Putnam Inc.,
375 Hudson Street, New York, New York 10014.
JOVE and the "J" design
are trademarks belonging to Penguin Putnam Inc.

PRINTED IN THE UNITED STATES OF AMERICA

10 9 8 7 6 5 4 3 2 1

Chapter 1

It was a crisp and windy October afternoon when Longarm climbed the stone steps of the Denver Federal Building. He wore his usual brown tweed suit, vest, blue-gray shirt and shoestring tie. It was so windy that he had to hold his flat-crowned Stetson down or it would have sailed off between the downtown buildings. The sky overhead was slate gray, and he knew that it would soon snow. There had been ice ringing the banks of Cherry Creek this morning that had not melted until mid-morning. Deputy Marshal Custis Long enjoyed winters so long as he didn't have to be on some cold and lonely outlaw train in the high, freezing country.

For the past week he'd been relaxing and recuperating from an especially difficult assignment up in Montana, where he'd been forced to track down and kill two outlaws who had taken the governor's daughter hostage. They'd demanded ten thousand dollars in small bills and threatened to kill the girl if they didn't get their money. Longarm had made sure that they'd each gotten one-way tickets straight to hell. It had been a tough and bloody job and he'd needed time off to pull himself together. Sometimes it seemed to Longarm as if he hardly ever had a chance to sit back and smell the roses anymore. Mostly, that was because his boss, Federal Marshal Billy Vail, chose him for the most dangerous and difficult jobs.

Well, Longarm thought, *I'm not going anywhere for at least a month and then it had better be south to warmer country.*

When he entered the federal building, Longarm was instantly engulfed by the kind of clerical confusion and political backbiting that he detested. Oh, there were some fine and dedicated employees here, many of whom he called friends. But then again, he had the luxury of rarely being around so that the gossipmongers had little ammunition to use against him.

"Afternoon, Custis," a pretty young woman by the name of Polly Raymond called, rushing across the lobby to grab his sleeve and then give him a peck on the cheek. "I've *really* missed you. Can we get together tonight?"

Longarm liked Polly. She was fun-loving and not the kind that kept badgering a man to get married. "I don't have any plans for this evening," he said, "unless Billy thinks otherwise."

"How long have you been back in town?"

"Not long."

Polly gave him a look that said she didn't believe it. "I'll bet you've been here for at least a couple of days. You probably have some other girls on a string. And here I thought that I was your favorite."

"You are," he said. "I'll come by at seven and pick you up for supper. We'll have steaks and good whiskey."

"I'd love to do that," Polly said, glancing around the big, marble-sided lobby and noticing that more than a few of her co-workers were watching them with either envy or amusement. "Custis," she added, "I had better get back to work. Don't forget about our date tonight!"

"Not a chance," he vowed, making a note to come up with some excuse for Lola about why he would not be able to take her out this evening. As Polly hurried off, Longarm watched her wiggle with unconcealed admiration, knowing the delights that were waiting until after they had dinner and went back to her apartment.

A fellow deputy marshal named George Avery stopped, nudged Custis in the ribs and complained, "You lucky dog. I've been trying to get a date with Polly for months but she's always too busy. What the hell do you have that I don't?"

Longarm turned his attention to the man who, at five-foot-eight, was at least eight inches shorter and thirty pounds heavier than himself. "George, I'm sure that I couldn't guess."

"Me neither," the man growled. "I even own a home. Hell, I'll bet you don't own much more than the clothes and the gun you wear. I hear you spend your money as fast as you make it."

"That's right," Custis said good-naturedly. "In my line of work, saving for tomorrow just doesn't seem like the smart thing to do."

"Well," George huffed, "we're *both* deputy marshals."

"I know," Longarm replied. "But you're best riding a desk chair while I prefer a horse . . . or a pretty woman."

Avery wasn't listening and so he missed the jibe. His hungry, beady little eyes were locked on Polly's swaying caboose. He sighed. "I sure wish she'd let me show her my house and the size of my bank account. Maybe then she'd realize that looks ain't everything when it comes to picking a man."

"Well," Longarm said, "your day with Miss Raymond may come yet . . . but I doubt it."

Avery heard him this time and his face darkened with jealous indignation. "You think you're so damned important. Well, you ain't! Some day I expect to be your boss and then that smirk on your face will disappear."

Longarm had no time or patience for this frustrated lit-

3

tle man. Not wanting to lose his temper or waste words, he simply walked off, leaving George Avery standing in the middle of the lobby. He mounted the stairs and went straight to Billy Vail's office.

"Come on in, Custis!" his boss called. "And close the door behind you."

Billy's office wasn't plush or showy, but the man sure liked to put pictures, plaques, and things all over his walls and desk. He was obviously a man who liked permanence and his office reflected the major events and items important in his life. Everywhere you looked you noted Billy's awards, the gifts that he'd received from his loving wife and children. Longarm's own small cubicle was nearly empty; he had no use for possessions and mementos that tended to tie a man down and make him believe that sitting behind a desk surrounded by four walls all day wasn't really so bad.

"Billy, how have you been?" he asked, settling into a chair and leaning back with his boots outstretched.

"I've been fine." Billy shuffled some papers. It seemed to Longarm that his boss was always shuffling paperwork. "Have you recovered from Montana yet?"

"I have."

Billy was a short, balding and popular man with a congenial air. Unlike George Avery, Billy harbored no jealousy toward Longarm either for his size or for his good looks. Billy had spent his time out in the field too. He was a man who'd earned the right to sit behind a desk and delegate assignments. Billy did his work well and let the cards fall where they might, knowing that he'd survive the office politics. He might never be top dog in this office jungle, but neither would he ever be fired. Longarm knew that Billy had the rest of his life figured out as well as the size of his investments and eventual government pension due when he retired in about ten more years.

"So," Billy said, offering Longarm a cigar, which he

4

accepted and then put into his coat pocket to enjoy that evening, "what have you been doing this past week?"

"I've been sleeping and eating well."

"You look much more rested," Billy said. "When you returned from Montana, I thought you'd been dragged through a wringer and hung out wet to dry."

"Tracking and killing those two kidnappers wasn't the easiest assignment I've ever had," Longarm admitted. "I was just sure that they would kill that girl before I could get them in my gun sights."

"The governor was very, very pleased with the work you did up there in Montana. He had his own people working on it, but you're the fella that delivered. He'd like to hire you as a special assistant, Custis."

"Montana is a little too cold and lonesome for me. I prefer Colorado and working for you."

Billy grinned and scratched his potbelly. "Thanks."

"How is your family?" Longarm asked, knowing that there was nothing that Billy would rather talk about than his wife and children.

"They're all fine. The boys are growing like weeds, and I swear my daughter is going to be so pretty that I'll have to beat her future beaus off with a club."

They both chuckled, then Billy asked, "Why don't you come over for supper tonight?"

"I'll have to take a rain check."

"Who is she this time?" Billy asked, leaning forward and giving Longarm a conspiratorial wink.

"Never mind," Longarm told his friend. "You'll probably find out anyway with all the wagging tongues because she works in this building."

Billy waved his hand in a gesture of contempt. "Aw hell, Custis, you know I never listen to the office gossip."

"That's to your credit." Longarm started to add something, but suddenly the door to Billy's office flew open as a wild-looking man waving a gun jumped into the room

5

and slammed and locked the door behind him.

Longarm's blood turned to ice. He didn't recognize the derelict that stood before them with a gun barrel wagging back and forth like an avenging finger of death. But he knew from the crazed look in the man's eyes that he meant to use this gun and kill them both.

"Easy!" Billy shouted, his face turning pale. "Don't shoot!"

The ragged scarecrow shrieked, "Don't you move . . . either of you . . . or by thunder you'll soon be dancing with the devil!"

Longarm wore his .44-40 Colt on his hip but, sitting down, it was going to be a slow job of getting it free. Much better, he thought, to use his hideout pistol, a small but deadly .44 derringer that was attached to his Ingersol railroad watch and chain. The derringer was resting in his vest pocket and Longarm began to slide his hand in that direction.

"Hands over your head right now or I'll shoot you both!" the man cried.

Longarm knew that he'd never stand a chance of getting the derringer out in time to save both himself and Billy so he raised his hands, praying for a diversion or some other means of getting the drop on this man.

Billy Vail cleared his throat and, when he spoke, his voice sounded remarkably composed. "Sir, have I or my deputy done something to offend you? Because, if we have, we are sincerely sorry. Perhaps it would be best if we calmly discussed your grievance."

With his free hand, the armed man reached into his coat pocket and dragged out a pint bottle of whiskey. Uncorking it with the aid of his rotting teeth, he drank deeply, eyes and gun never leaving his captives.

"Ugggh," he choked, then wiped his eyes. "There ain't nothing in this world that's worth anything except whiskey."

6

"I'm glad you enjoy it," Longarm said, trying to keep the conversation going and buy time. "Do I know you?"

The filthy stranger wagged his head and took another pull on his bottle.

Longarm's eyes shifted over to Billy and he said, "Then you must know this . . . uh, gentleman."

Billy managed a smile. "I'm not sure that I've had the . . . uh . . . pleasure. Mister, have we met before?"

"Nope."

Billy's eyebrows shot up. "Then what reason have you to threaten our lives?"

The stranger was dressed in rags. He was emaciated and unshaven. Longarm was sure that he had neither bathed nor slept in a bed for days, perhaps even for weeks. Longarm knew this wasn't the only man who prowled the streets of Denver, half-crazed and without a home or a friend, but he might well be the most dangerous. The one that finally punched his own ticket after so many years of swapping lead with outlaws all over the West.

The man's eyes were ringed with darkness and his beard was stained by liquor and tobacco. He took another long, shuddering swig of whiskey and then croaked, "I come to make a confession and you'd by damned better listen to it well!"

"We're not clergy," Billy said in his most soothing voice.

"What!" the stranger cried.

"You know, ministers. We are lawmen, not men of God."

The fellow blinked and then seemed to understand and take offense. Waving the gun at them, he cried, "Mister, I ain't here to make a confession for my gawdamn soul! I'm a sinner and I'm going to hell, of that I am certain. Nothing can change that fact."

"Maybe what you need is a doctor," Longarm suggested. "You might not be feeling too well right now."

The stranger's eyes widened and then he threw back his head and guffawed. Laughed as if Longarm had said the funniest thing imaginable.

Finally regaining his composure, the wild man's haunted eyes narrowed and he said, "How would *you* feel if you had the blood of five innocent people on your head? Five murders staining your soul and filling your nights with ghosts so hideous that you were sure you were about to go completely insane?"

"I'd feel awful," Longarm said simply. "But we still don't have any idea why you have burst into this office and threatened to kill us. In what possible way have we offended you, stranger?"

The man took a deep breath. He was swaying on his feet and Longarm thought he might even collapse. Instead, he said in a gravelly voice, "I come here to make my peace with the law. You're both the law, ain't ya?"

"Yes, but . . ."

"Then I'll tell you straight out what I come for and . . ."

There was a knock on the door. "Mr. Vail, is everything all right in there?" a man called. "I heard shouting and . . ."

"If he comes through that door, I'll kill him," the stranger hissed in warning.

"It's just fine in here," Billy called out. "Go back to work."

"All right," the voice said sounding dubious. "But . . ."

"I'm fine!" Billy shouted, putting some anger in his voice. "Now don't interrupt us again!"

Whoever it was left. The derelict swallowed hard. He was shaking as if he had chills and fever. Longarm was afraid that the gun in his hand would go off by accident. "Maybe," he said, "you should put that Colt down on the desk. Then we can all relax."

"I don't care if you relax or not!" the man shouted. "I

ain't had a moment of peace in seven years. So why should I care if your mind is at rest?"

Right then, Longarm was sure that this mad stranger was going to start firing. His hand inched closer to the derringer in his vest pocket and just as he was about to make a grab for the weapon, the derelict turned his face to the ceiling and cried, "Forgive me, Lord!"

Then, he placed the barrel of his Colt to his temple and cocked back the hammer.

"Wait!" Billy shouted. "Don't do that!"

The man raised up on his toes. "God," he wailed, "I don't deserve it, but please forgive me!"

Longarm watched the man begin to squeeze the trigger of the Colt revolver. He jumped out of his chair and dove straight at the stranger hoping to knock the gun from his hand before he blew out his whiskey-soaked brains. Longarm's shoulder slammed into the man's stomach but his gun went off anyway. The stranger was as light as a scarecrow and they crashed to the floor. Longarm knew he'd deflected the gun, but not quite enough because the derelict was bleeding from a head wound and was dying.

"Get a doctor!" Longarm shouted. "And some bandages!"

Billy ran to his door, forgot it was locked, and lost precious seconds trying to get out into the hall. Longarm paid him no attention because the dying man was tugging on his string tie and desperately trying to speak.

"What is it?" Longarm asked. "What are you trying to tell me?"

The man's sunken eyes focused. They seemed as bright and as hard as diamonds and his voice was like the sound of dry twigs breaking when he asked, "Do you remember that bank job five years ago when eight innocent people were gunned down in cold blood?"

"Yes." Longarm remembered because he'd been in Denver at the time. He'd even gone to the scene of the

9

crime and despite years of seeing death and carnage, the scene inside that bank had left him feeling as if he wanted to gag. And although the entire city had been outraged, the criminals, who had worn hoods, had gotten away with over twenty-five thousand dollars in cash. They'd left behind no witnesses, not even a boy who had been holding hands with his mother when he'd been executed.

"I was one of the fellas that took the money."

"What's your name?" Longarm asked.

"Joe Gorney."

"Who were the others and what happened to the bank's money?" Longarm knew that this man was very near death and that he held the key to solving those brutal murders. "Tell me!"

Gorney fought for breath. "The leader was a big, red-haired fellow named Jude. No . . . no last name!"

"What about the others?"

"There was Hugh Bain. Mad Dog Trabert. Carl Appleby and . . . Mando Lopez. I was outside with the horses but I could hear the screams and gunshots." The dying man tried to pull Longarm even closer. "I swear that I didn't know that they were going to murder everyone in that bank. I thought we was just going to rob it!"

"Where are those men now?"

The dying man tried to answer but his body convulsed and his heels began to pound the polished office floor. Longarm looked to the door and shouted, "We need a doctor!"

Billy ran back inside. "There's one being sent for. Who is he? What is he trying to say?"

Before Longarm could answer, Joe Gorney croaked, "I swear that I never knew that Jude intended to murder all those people. There were even women and children in that bank. God, forgive me!"

Billy grabbed Longarm. "Is he talking about that—"

10

"Yes," Longarm interrupted. "This poor devil was the bank holdup gang's lookout."

Longarm leaned closer. The man's head was now haloed in a widening pool of blood and it was amazing that he was still alive, much less able to make his dying confession.

"Mister, can you tell me anything else? Anything at all that would help me find those men and that bank money?"

"I never even got my share of the loot!" Gorney's whole body was shaking. "I . . . I am so sorry! Get 'em, Marshal! Kill every last one of the bloody . . ."

Gorney wasn't able to finish. A deep death rattle sounded in his lungs, his heels stopped beating the floor and his body went limp.

Longarm and Billy stared at each other for a long moment, and then Billy asked, "Was he able to give you the names of those murderers?"

"Yes."

Billy jumped up and ran to his desk. He returned a moment later with a pad and pencil. "Write them down now, Custis. Write them down before you forget."

"I was there at the bank just after the slaughter," Longarm told his boss and friend. "I would never forget those names."

"I know, but write them down anyway!"

But Longarm hesitated. "I want to go after them myself."

"This is no time to . . ."

"I'm not asking," Longarm said, lips compressed in a hard line. "I'm the only one who knows the names of those killers. If I tell you then you'll have to tell your boss, and that means that it will get leaked to the press and we may never bring the gang to justice."

Billy stood up. "All right. I'll go along with you because you're right. But I have to insist on one condition."

"And that is?"

"I also have to know the names that man gave you as he was dying."

"Why?"

"Because, if I don't and you're killed . . . then those murderers will certainly never be caught."

"I won't get killed."

"Be reasonable," Billy said softly. "I also saw those victims. If you are killed, I swear that I'll strap on my old six-gun and go after that bunch myself."

Longarm's friend was shaking with fury and conviction. And while Billy had grown soft in his desk chair, he was also still a man to be reckoned with and feared.

"All right," Longarm agreed. "I'll give you the names before I start my investigation and track-down. But they'll be our secret until those five men are either dead . . . or brought to justice."

"Five? I thought witnesses said there were six."

"There were," Longarm said. "But this poor, crazed sonofabitch was one of them."

"Yeah," Billy said, passing his hand across his face and taking a deep, steadying breath. "I see what you mean."

Chapter 2

When Longarm left the federal building, everyone was in a panic. No one noticed him slip out the door and head down the street while imprinting the names of five killers indelibly on his mind. He'd provided Billy with those same names, but Longarm knew that bringing in the bank robbers and murderers was his job. Billy had told him to do whatever it took and not to worry about time or expenses. Neither of them believed that, after five years, any of the stolen money would be recovered, but there were wounds that would never heal until the killers had been brought to justice. A hangman's noose . . . or a bullet, it just didn't matter to Longarm one way or the other.

Not sure of where to begin picking up a five-year-old trail, he headed for the seediest part of Denver. Down near the train- and stockyards where the saloons served bad, watered-down whiskey, the prostitutes were armed and poisonous and a man's life wasn't worth a plug nickel. Longarm was not too optimistic about the chances of one or more of the bank killers still being in Denver, but he didn't know anyplace better to start his investigation.

He was well known in the worst parts of Denver as a hard man, but a fair one. And now, as Longarm strode into an especially notorious and seedy saloon called the Bulldog, the owner's head shot up and the man forced a frozen smile.

"Marshal Custis Long," he said, loud enough for everyone in the place to be warned about their wagging lips, "what a pleasure. Can I pour you a glass of whiskey?"

"No, thanks. Brice, I'd like to talk to you for a minute in private."

"Well," the man said, wiping his bar with a filthy rag, "I'm a little busy right now. As you can see, I've got business."

Longarm glared at the five or six tough-looking customers standing next to the bar. "Any of you men mind if I take him away for a few minutes?"

They didn't like him and they didn't like honoring a request of any kind but they had no choice, and so they reluctantly wagged their heads back and forth.

"Good," Longarm said, motioning for Brice to follow him over to the saloon's most remote table. "Sit down," Longarm said, drawing up a battered chair.

"Thanks," Brice replied, his voice cryptic. He was a fat man and gently eased his bulk into a chair that looked incapable of holding his considerable weight. "Marshal Long, what can I do for you today?"

"Maybe I can do something for you," Longarm said.

"Oh, I doubt that."

Longarm saw three cigars protruding from the saloon owner's shirt pocket. He reached across the table and plucked one out, then examined it in the dim light. "Are these any good?"

"The best that Virginia has to offer. Help yourself."

"Don't mind if I do." Longarm bit the tip off the cigar, then searched his pockets for a match. Finding none, he looked across the table.

"Here," Brice said, striking a match and lighting the cigar. "What else do you want from me today?"

14

Longarm inhaled and then exhaled smoke. "I need your help."

Brice chuckled obscenely. "You need *my* help?"

"That's right."

"In what way?"

"Do you remember that bank holdup five years ago when eight innocent victims were gunned down in cold blood?"

"Sure." The saloon owner's expression turned sour. "I thought the town was going to come apart. There were gangs of vigilantes in the streets. Some of them came marching through this neighborhood and it got ugly. Me and a couple of customers had to stand them off with shotguns. They were threatening to burn this whole block down!"

"There was at least twenty-five thousand dollars taken that day and neither the money . . . or the killers were ever found."

"I know that. So what has this got to do with me helping you?"

"Today," Longarm said, speaking slowly and with great emphasis, "one of the gang members was shot to death."

Brice was the kind of rough-hewn man who had, in his fifty-odd years, probably seen about everything vile that existed in this world. Longarm had no doubt that the saloon owner had killed and robbed men and gotten away with it more than once. But he also had no doubt that the kind of men that Brice preyed upon were the kind that preyed upon the innocent.

"So I repeat," the saloon owner said, "what does it have to do with me?"

"Before the man died, he made a confession. He told me the names of the other gang members. I'm here, looking for them."

Brice shook his head. "Marshal, you're barking up the

15

wrong tree. I don't know anything about that bank robbery or those murders. I swear it."

"Maybe you do and maybe you don't."

Even in the poor light, Longarm could see the man's face darken with anger. "I just said . . ."

"Hold your voice down," Longarm warned. "I'm not here to arrest you or to cause you any grief. But I thought that you might have heard or seen something about the time of the robberies that left you suspicious."

"I saw nothing." Brice stroked his sagging chins. "I heard absolutely nothing."

Longarm pretended not to be listening. "The kind of men that would execute innocent women and children are the kind that come into your Bulldog Saloon. Maybe a few days after the bank robbery, a man or even several men suddenly had money to spend. Big money."

"Now why would they come in here if they had 'big money?' " Brice shot back. "You know that I only serve losers."

"Habit," Longarm said. "Men drink around others like themselves. I'm just asking you to think back five years and try to come up with a name or two."

"I can't help you."

Longarm blew smoke in the fat man's face. "I got a feeling that you haven't tried."

"And you," Brice said, his voice hardening, "haven't told me why I *should* try. What's in it for me, Marshal? Nothing is for free. You know that as well as I do."

"What's in it for you," Longarm answered, "is a reward."

"How much?"

Longarm shrugged. "I don't know, but it will probably be ten percent. That would be twenty-five hundred. Plus, you'd be a hero in Denver. People would want you to make speeches and ride a float on the Fourth of July."

16

"Ha! Now that would be something! Me, a hero." Brice laughed. "Me, a *respected* citizen."

"Think about it, Brice. You'd have almost free rein to operate without harassment from the city. Lawmen like myself might even look the other way when you crossed the line but caused no real harm."

The man's smile disappeared and a look of cunning crept into his deep-set eyes. "Marshal Long, are you saying I could break the laws?"

"I'm saying that everyone in Denver with any authority . . . including myself . . . would view you as a man who proved himself honorable and helped to right a terrible wrong. You'd be feted, and you might also be twenty-five hundred dollars richer."

"And I might be dead," Brice replied. "The people that did that bank job aren't the kind to waste time slapping a man around, Marshal. Whoever fingers them had damn sure better write out his last will and testament."

"Not if I kill or arrest them first." Longarm pushed to his feet. "If you can remember anything, you'll be well repaid."

Brice also came to his feet. "Like I said, I don't remember a thing except that a bunch of self-righteous citizens of Denver came marching down our street with torches in their hands and murder in their hearts."

Longarm shrugged. "You know where to find me if you suddenly remember anything important."

Brice opened his mouth to say something, then closed it.

"What?" Longarm demanded.

"Actually, now that I think about it, I *do* remember a regular customer who suddenly had a lot of money about that time," Brice said, voice dropping as he squeezed his bulk back down in the groaning chair again.

"Go on!"

"But he said he'd inherited it. And he spent it all inside of six months."

17

"Does this man still come around?"

"Not for quite a while. And the last time he was in here he didn't say much and he sure didn't buy any more whiskey on the house."

"What's his name?"

Brice stared up through the cigar smoke. "I'm not sure I remember."

Longarm reached into his pocket and and slapped a twenty-dollar gold piece down on the table. "Think hard."

"I think his name was . . ." Brice's sausage-like fingers covered the coin, and when Longarm let it go, the man said, "Yes, it was Carl."

Longarm suddenly felt his heart began to beat faster. Joe Gorney had said that one of the bank robbers was named Carl Appleby. "What was his last name?"

"Be serious! No one here tells anyone their last names."

Longarm glanced over at the tough lineup of men at the bar and he could well believe it. "Where does Carl work?"

"I doubt he does work. But he once bragged that he was a muleskinner for one of the local freighting companies that hauled supplies between Denver and Central City. Said he was quitting, though."

"Maybe he went back to work after he spent his share of the bank holdup money."

"That would be a lot of dough."

Longarm nodded in agreement. "Yes, but we both know that a fool can be parted from his wealth in a hurry. Maybe you and your girls even took some of it. Huh?"

"I don't know anything about any bank money!"

"All right, I believe you. What does Carl look like?"

Brice motioned toward the bar. "You see them boys belly up to my bar waiting to have their glasses refilled? Carl looks like any and all of them, only he smelled like a mule . . . brayed like one too . . . when he laughed, which wasn't often."

18

"How tall? How big? What age? And tell me if he has any scars or marks that I can recognize when I find him."

"He's as tall as you are," Brice said, looking impatient to get back to his customers. "But not as big. He's a thin man with a full beard."

"That doesn't help much."

"The beard has some silver in it because Carl is probably in his late forties. He has real bad teeth and I think that he is hard of hearing."

"Hard of hearing?"

"That's right. I remember people had to yell at him before he'd answer. But it often gets real loud in here so everyone has to yell back and forth to be heard."

"What kind of clothes did he wear?"

Brice shrugged. "Carl dressed like a muleskinner. He wore suspenders. Red ones, I recall."

"Did he pack a sidearm?"

"No," Brice said. "But I remember he wore a Bowie knife on his belt. Yeah. In a real fancy beaded buckskin sheath."

"Like an Indian would make?"

"That's right. And he had plenty of knife scars on his face, hands and forearms."

"Now we're getting somewhere," Longarm said, feeling his excitement rise. "How bad were these scars?"

"One of them was across the point of his jaw and up into his lower lip. It gave him a little bit of an odd look. I mean, you were never sure if Carl was smiling, scowling . . . or if it was just that lip scar."

"Was he missing any fingers?"

"No," Brice decided after several moments' consideration. "But his hands were really ugly. Lots of scars. You only had to look at his hands to know that he had been in some bad knife fights and he wasn't one to be crossed."

"Anything else?"

19

"No. Marshal, if you catch him, how soon will I get that twenty-five-hundred-dollar reward?"

"I can't say," Longarm told the man. "I don't even know for sure if there will be a reward."

Brice's eyes widened. "Dammit, you said . . ."

"I said that there will *probably* be a reward offered by the bank for the arrest and conviction of the murderers and the recovery of their money."

"But it will all be spent by now!" Brice shouted.

"Yeah," Longarm said, trying to look sympathetic. "I'm afraid so."

Brice shook with anger. "Dammit, will you at least carry through on your promise to tell the mayor and everyone else who gives me a bad time to lay off because I cooperated?"

"I will," Longarm agreed. Figuring that he'd gotten all that he could from the saloon owner, Longarm blew a cloud over Brice and drawled, "Actually, these are pretty good cigars."

"Of course. I told you that I order them from the state of Virginia. They're as good as Cubans."

"Not quite, but close." Longarm started to leave. "I'll keep in touch. And if Carl comes back, you just send someone down to the federal building with a note for Marshal Custis Long to come around. It'll get to me."

Brice didn't look a bit happy. "I feel like I've been lied to," he complained. "I did what you asked and then you tell me there probably won't even be a reward."

"Life is hard and almost never fair," Longarm told him. "But I do appreciate and I won't forget your help."

"Sure."

Longarm left the saloon and strolled along smoking Brice's Virginia cigar. He would hit every other saloon on this street and then he'd visit every freight office in town. It would take time and if he came up with nothing, he'd take a stage up to Central City and go looking for Carl.

20

Chapter 3

Longarm visited every other saloon in that rough section of town, and it was evening when he recalled that he was supposed to pick up Polly and take her out to dinner. He'd be late, and the grimness of the suicide and the murder investigation had left him in poor spirits. Actually, he wanted to visit other saloons on the off chance that he might come up with more leads. Maybe even connect with other members of the gang. After all, Carl Appleby was only one of the killers. There were still Hugh Bain, Mad Dog Trabert, Mando Lopez and the gang's mysterious leader to think about.

But Longarm had made a promise to Polly and he knew that she would still be waiting. "I smell like a brewery," he muttered, hurrying off toward her apartment. "No, it's worse than that . . . I smell like I've been cleaning pigpens all day."

It was nearly nine o'clock when he knocked on Polly Raymond's door. It opened almost immediately. She was dressed for an evening on the town and when she saw Longarm in his messed-up clothes, she exclaimed, "Custis! Where have you been?"

"On a murder investigation."

21

"I heard you were with that man who shot himself in Mr. Vail's office. Did it have anything to do with him?"

"Sort of, but I can't talk about that."

Polly's hand flew to her nose. "Phew! You smell awful!"

"I know," he said, hat in hand. "Maybe we ought to postpone dinner tonight. I have to—"

"Come on inside," she interrupted, grabbing his hand and dragging him through her doorway. "I'll run a bath and you can clean up."

"My clothes will still smell bad."

"Hmmm," she said. "Well, we can eat here this evening and you don't have to wear them."

"Oh?"

Polly shot off toward the other room to prepare hot water for his bath. "It'll be fine!" she called.

Longarm removed his hat, then his coat and finally his vest. He sat down and pulled off his boots and then his pants until he was down to his underclothes. "If you say so," he yelled.

Polly appeared with a bucket of water to be heated on her stove. Glancing across the room, she said, "You've lost some weight, Custis."

"Montana can be hard on a man."

"I've got chicken and dumplings and apple pie for desert."

"It sounds great." Longarm got up and went to give Polly a hug of appreciation.

"Not until you've bathed," she said, retreating. "I'm serious. You smell just awful!"

Longarm shrugged. He spied a newspaper on her sofa and went over to read it while he waited for the water to heat. It was too early for there to be any mention of the suicide that had just taken place in the Denver Federal Building. And even when that news was published, there wouldn't be any real information of value. Billy Vail would never break his promise to keep the circumstances surrounding the death of Joe Gorney their own little secret.

Polly came over with a glass of whiskey. "You look like you really could use a drink."

He took the glass. "Thanks. It's been a tough day."

"That was terrible about that poor man killing himself. Why did he come to Mr. Vail's office?"

"He had something to say," Longarm said, purposefully vague.

"Did you know him?"

"No."

"Then he must have known Mr. Vail."

"I guess," Longarm said. "How long will it take that water to heat?"

"Not more than five minutes."

Longarm slumped down on the sofa. "There are times when I think I should have been a banker or a businessman of some kind instead of a federal marshal."

Polly sat down close to him. "It was that bad, huh?"

"Yeah," he said. "And things didn't get much better after I left."

"I wish you could tell me what this is all about."

"Well," Longarm said, "I suppose it won't hurt to tell you a little about what I've gotten involved in. But it's confidential."

"Of course!"

"The man who shot himself in the head was a member of the gang that committed those murders during that big downtown bank robbery five years ago."

"He was?"

"That's right. His name was Joe Gorney. Apparently, he was not actually one of the shooters and, if he was to be believed, never even suspected that there would be any shooting. He just held the horses outside the bank. When the executions began, he was caught in the middle and had no choice but to ride for his life with the others."

"Do you believe that?"

"Yes, I do," Longarm answered. "The man had obviously been haunted by guilt and consumed by nightmares ever since the killings. He was ruined and drowning in misery. He came to make his confession and to tell us the names of the other gang members."

"He did?"

"Yes, but that's the part you can't tell anyone about. Only Billy Vail and I know those names and Billy has given me the responsibility of tracking the gang down and bringing them to justice."

"What . . ."

"Don't ask me their names because I won't tell you," Longarm said. "There's no reason for you to know."

"You're right," Polly agreed. "I don't want to know. But I am worried about you."

"Don't be. I haven't gotten any really good leads despite visiting every low-down saloon in Denver."

"Which explains why you smell so bad."

"That's right. The only lead I received was from the man who owns a saloon called the Bulldog. Brice thinks that a muleskinner might be one of the killers. He gave me a description, but it's one that will be hard to track."

"So what will you do now?"

"I'll follow that lead and I may have to go up to Central City." Longarm sighed. "Polly, I don't want to talk about this anymore."

She leaned over and gave him a kiss. "Even almost naked, you still smell awful. I'll get the bath ready as quick as I can and then supper."

"Thanks. I'm afraid that I'm not going to be much company this evening."

"I don't mind. Can you stay the night?"

"Are you sure you want me to, given the foul mood I'm in?"

"Of course. And besides, I might be able to improve that mood, if I try hard enough."

Longarm caught her drift. "Yeah," he said, "you might at that."

He took his bath and Polly used a straight razor to give him a good, close shave. She washed his hair and scrubbed his back and when he finally got out of the cast iron tub, she splashed something nice-smelling on his face, then toweled him down until he was aroused.

"You're good to me, Polly," he said, reaching for her as he stood naked beside the tub of dirty water.

"That's because you're good to me right back," she replied, coming into his arms and cupping his bare buttocks with both hands. "Mmmmm. You smell so much better now!"

"Why don't we detour the kitchen and head for your bedroom?"

"Before we eat?"

"Yeah," he said, feeling his manhood began to stiffen. "My mind isn't on food at the moment."

Polly reached for his manhood and gave it a gentle massage. "I can tell. All right."

She led Longarm into the bedroom and when he stretched out on her mattress, Polly took her time undressing because she had a beautiful body and knew he appreciated looking at her before they made love.

"You're taking a long time," he said.

"Anticipation is a big part of the fun."

"I'll tell you the one that anticipates having a night with you," Longarm said.

Polly looked over at him with interest. "Who?"

"George Avery. He's got it bad for you."

She dismissed this news with a wave of her hand. "Too bad that I find Marshal Avery so pushy and repulsive."

"The poor man wonders if you'd change your mind and

marry him if you knew he owned a house in town free and clear and had money in the bank."

"Next time you see George," Polly said, anger in her voice, "tell him to quit staring at me as if I were a piece of meat in a butcher shop. And I'm not the only one that feels that way. Some of the other girls say he practically drools when they walk by. And one of them swears that he *plays* with himself at his desk. Can't you ask Mr. Vail to transfer that love-starved slug to some other building?"

"I'm afraid that I don't carry much influence in the office."

"That's because you're never there. But if you were, you'd see how disgusting Marshal Avery can be around all young women. That's why his attentions aren't the least bit flattering."

Longarm nodded with understanding. Polly wasn't tall, maybe five-foot-three, but she was round in all the right places. She had a slim waist, perfect legs and breasts as delicious as sweet summer melons. "Come here," he ordered, reaching for her when the last of her undergarments slid to the floor.

Polly threw a leg over Longarm's powerful body and straddled him on the bed. "What's your pleasure?" she asked provocatively.

"Lean over and let me have a good taste of those beauties."

Polly was only too happy to oblige and when Longarm's lips found first one of her nipples and then the other, she moaned with satisfaction. Longarm sampled each until they were standing up and as firm and delicious as fresh strawberries.

"Custis, you do that better than any man I've ever met. Now let's do the best part."

Longarm started to roll her over and climb on top but Polly had other ideas. "Let me do it slow on top first," she said.

26

"Whatever you like pleases me."

Polly grabbed his stiff member and moved it gently back and forth against the soft, pink lips of her womanhood. Eyes glazed with pleasure and breath coming faster, she rubbed the head of his manhood against the bud of her own fountainhead until she began to moan.

"Good, huh?" he asked, a big grin on his face.

"It's wonderful," she replied. "There's nothing like the feel of it in this world."

"Yeah," he agreed, bumping his hips upward so that his throbbing tool penetrated her a few inches. "They were made for each other."

Polly must have thought so too because she rocked her hips forward and swallowed his member completely, pressing her hips tight against his own. "Don't move," she whispered. "Just stay still for a moment while I feel you so far up inside me."

Longarm placed his hands on her hips. After a few minutes when he couldn't stand it any longer, he began to ease her hips up and down, then around and around. He liked to watch her face and see how much pleasure she was receiving, and from the smile he saw, Longarm knew that Polly was enjoying this every bit as much as himself.

"It's like you're stirring me," she dreamily whispered, eyes closed. "Like you've got a big spoon and it's churning around and around inside me so that I can't feel or even think of anything but the place where we are coming together."

Longarm chuckled. "I'll be your spoon if that's what you want to think. But my spoon is going to turn into a big fire hose pretty quick."

Polly bent over and kissed his mouth, then rolled off Longarm so that he could mount her. When he did, she wrapped her legs around his waist and hugged him tightly. "Just don't stop. Don't ever stop."

"That's not possible," he said. "But I'm in no hurry."

Polly began to suck on his neck and Longarm began to stir her faster and faster until she threw her head back and howled with delight.

"I'm coming, Custis! Come on! Faster. Harder. Oh, oh yes!"

She lost control as great waves of pleasure surged through her lovely little body. Her legs waved at the ceiling and her eyes widened as they might have if she'd seen something extraordinary appear on the ceiling. Then she locked her legs around his waist again and her body demanded every last drop of his creamy, hot seed.

They had supper and went to bed to make love a second time. When Longarm fell asleep that night, he felt more relaxed than when he'd arrived. Polly Raymond was his favorite girl. And if he were a marrying kind of man he'd probably ask her to tie the knot.

Chapter 4

When Longarm and Polly arrived at the federal building the next morning, they acted as if they'd just met on the outside steps.

"Custis," she whispered, her face a little flushed and whisker-burned, "my legs still feel shaky from all the lovemaking we did last night."

"And I feel like a stallion."

"I'll see you tonight."

"Yeah," he agreed. "But I might be late. I've got to finish covering all the saloons and . . . if I come across any leads I might not be able to come over to see you at all."

"I understand." Polly squeezed his hand and walked into the building.

Longarm paused to watch her hips swaying under her dress thinking, *If George Avery knew what he was missing with Polly, the* poor *bastard would probably slit his throat.*

He went straight up to Billy's office and when he stuck his head in the door, Billy looked up and said, "Come on in and shut the door behind you."

Longarm took a seat and tried to stifle a yawn.

"Rough night?" Billy asked.

"No, sir."

"You look a lot wearier than you did yesterday."

"I had a full day and evening after Joe Gorney shot himself."

"Yeah, I'll just bet you did," Billy said, leaning back in his office chair. "But what I want to know is if you did anything *productive*."

"Yesterday afternoon I visited more run-down saloons than I can remember," Longarm told the man.

"Any luck?"

"Maybe." Longarm told him about what he'd learned from Brice at the Bulldog Saloon and ended by saying, "It's not a great lead, but it's the best I've come up with so far."

"It sounds good to me. I wish I could assign a couple of men to help you on this one. It would sure hurry things along."

"I know," Longarm said, "but you can't without telling them why they'd be searching for an aging knife fighter named Carl Appleby. Billy, just give me a few more days and I think I can find that man if he is still alive and working either here or up in Central City."

"Can I help you some way?"

Longarm shook his head. "It's a one-man investigation. Trust me, Billy. No one wants to see this case solved any more than I do."

"The relatives of the eight deceased might argue that point."

"I'm going to find Carl or one of the others before the week is out," Longarm vowed.

"Maybe you ought to go back to the Bulldog and have another talk with Brice. He might have remembered something else that would prove helpful."

"Good idea." Longarm paused. "Billy, I told him that there might be a reward for information leading to the arrest of the gang and the recovery of the money."

Billy scowled. "I doubt there will be since the money has almost certainly been spent over the past five years."

"I had to offer some kind of a carrot. I suggested that the reward could be as high as ten percent . . . twenty-five hundred dollars."

"That's ridiculous!"

Longarm shrugged his broad shoulders. "Maybe so, but it got me my first lead. I also told him he would be a hero if he helped me bring those murderers to justice. That he might even be asked to ride on Denver's Fourth of July float as a big celebrity."

Billy snorted with derision. "That's absurd! I know Brice and he's scum. Fat, pond-sucking scum. Why, he's so huge he'd probably even break the float wagon's axle!"

Longarm couldn't help but chuckle. "At any rate, should Brice come by here and ask for you, don't be abrupt or rude. I need the man's full cooperation. He might even know a thing or two about some of the other gang members. He's shrewd and crafty and not the kind to lay all his cards on the table at once."

"I follow you," Billy said, nodding his head. "So what are you going to do today . . . that is, if you feel up to it after a long night with Miss Raymond."

Longarm smiled a little sheepishly. "I forgot that I'd mentioned we were going to supper last evening."

"Did you even take the time to eat before jumping into bed?"

"Billy, I'm a gentleman and gentlemen don't talk about their women."

"Sure. Sure," Billy said, not sounding the least bit impressed. "So what's your agenda today?"

"I'm going to visit the remaining saloons in Denver. Today it will be the better ones."

"Keep me posted. The head of our agency was all over me yesterday about that suicide and I had to do some fast

31

talking in order to keep our little secret. If Mr. Ludlow ever finds out that I'm holding back on him . . . it could be my job."

"He won't," Longarm vowed. "When I start making the arrests, I'll just say that I got an anonymous tip about the bank robbers. And I'll leave it at that without saying a word about poor Joe Gorney."

At the mention of the derelict's name, Billy's face clouded. "It's really something how that man was haunted to death by those murders. Did you believe him?"

"Yes, I did," Longarm replied. "That's not to say that poor Joe Gorney wasn't just as guilty as the other members of the holdup gang. He deserved to hang. But even so, I don't think he ever expected Jude and the others to execute everyone in that bank."

"Me neither."

Longarm plucked another cigar from Billy's shirt pocket and headed for the door.

"Don't forget to keep me posted on anything that turns up. And I mean *anything!*"

"I won't," Longarm called back, his mind already fixed on all the saloons, dance halls and gambling dens he'd have to visit this day. The bad part was that all his visits and questions about a five-year-old bank robbery would raise a lot of suspicions. And, if one or more of the gang were still in town, the word would get back to them that Denver's most feared deputy marshal was back on their trail.

Longarm was methodical. He had a street map of Denver fixed in his mind and he worked the downtown like a grid, not missing a single cross street and even entering a few more seedy places set back in the alleyways.

His approach was also consistent. He didn't drink when he entered an establishment but instead asked to see the owner. If that person wasn't available, he spoke to the bartender but only after establishing that the man had been in this same job five years earlier when the Bank of Colorado had been robbed. If the bartender was new, Longarm didn't ask any further questions.

He got nowhere with his questioning and was growing discouraged until about seven o'clock that evening when he was almost ready to quit. The small breakthrough happened at a saloon called Tony's Place. It was a popular hangout for a lot of the government workers and was only a block from the Denver Mint on Colfax. Longarm had been there many times and so was recognized the moment he walked in the door. He'd saved Tony's Place for the last, figuring he'd have a drink or two before heading on over to Polly's apartment.

The owner of the establishment was Tony Olmo, a handsome Italian in his sixties who charmed everyone yet still had the authority to keep out the troublemakers. There were never any brawls at Tony's Place because it was a posted policy that anyone who started raising hell and causing a ruckus would be banned from the popular saloon for life.

"Hey, Tony," Longarm called out. "How about the usual?"

"My pleasure, Marshal."

"And if you've got a few minutes to spare I need to have a few words with you in private."

"Sure thing," the Italian said, motioning to his younger brother who was the usual bartender. "We can sit over there by the back door. Nobody will bother us. I hope that I haven't had any complaints about our business."

"No complaints at all."

Tony looked relieved.

Tony's brother, Mario, brought them drinks. They exchanged pleasantries for a few moments before the bartender went back to work leaving Longarm and Tony to talk in private.

"Tony, I'm working on that old bank robbery," Long-arm began. "The one that took place five years ago when eight people were viciously murdered."

"Yeah, I remember." The Italian's handsome face turned sad. "Who could forget? You guys never even got a lead on that bunch, huh?"

"Not until yesterday."

Tony leaned forward, dark eyes suddenly intense. Lowering his voice even though they could not have been overheard, he whispered, "Is that what you want to talk about?"

"Yeah." Longarm sipped his whiskey. It was as good as any you'd find in town. Tony served nothing but the best to his friends. "I'm going to give you a name or two and you tell me if any of them are familiar."

"You have the names of those murderers!" Tony whispered, not bothering to hide his excitement.

"I didn't say that."

"No, you didn't but . . ."

Longarm held up his hand. "Tony, these names can't be repeated to anyone and I'm not saying they were part of that holdup. They're just names. Let's pretend that I'm making them up but hoping at least one of them is familiar."

"Sure." Tony winked. "I get it. Okay."

"You ever heard of a man named Joe Gorney?"

"No."

"What about Mando Lopez?"

"Uh-uh." Tony couldn't hide his disappointment.

"Carl Appleby?"

"No, I'm sorry."

"How about Hugh Bain or a fella nicknamed Mad Dog?"

"Would his last name be Trabert?" Tony asked, leaning forward.

Longarm took another drink and forced his voice to

34

stay calm. "I can't say. Just answer the question. Do you know anyone called Mad Dog?"

"It's not an uncommon nickname, Marshal. I've known a man named Bad Dog, but also a Mad Dog."

"Tell me about the one that you know as Mad Dog."

Tony took a drink and considered the question carefully before answering. "He's Irish and says he was a famous prizefighter back in New York. I'd say he's about your height and quite a lady's man. He's a handsome dog and he came here a long time ago wanting me to bankroll him in the fight game."

"You mean to be his manager?"

"Yes, but in the back alley. He said he could whip any man in Denver and I felt he was telling the truth. I wouldn't have wanted to fight him for any amount of money."

"Pretty tough, huh?"

"An *animal*," Tony swore. "And I'd heard of Mad Dog even before he came into my place looking for some fight money and management. I'd heard he went crazy in fights and had to be pulled off his victims otherwise he'd either kill or maim them for life. Quite frankly, the man scared me."

"So what happened when you refused to take his offer?"

"He found someone else. I heard that he went to the Bulldog and that the owner, Brice, backed him. Heard that he made quite a bit of money for Brice, but then he went crazy and beat an opponent to death and disappeared when he heard vigilantes were looking for him with a hangman's noose."

"Brice backed him, huh?"

"That's right. The man owns a little hellhole of a saloon over on—"

"I know the place," Longarm interrupted. "You ever have a customer named *Jude*?"

35

Tony shook his head. "Last name?"

"I don't have one."

"I can't help you with that name," Tony said. "But I sure remember Mad Dog Trabert."

"Would you have any idea what happened to him?"

"Nope. But someone ought to remember where he went because he was the kind of man that stood out in any crowd. He wasn't a bald man, but he shaved his skull real close and it was as scarred as his ugly mug. I'm told he would ram the top of his head into an opponent's face and break it up . . . the face, I mean. He was a wild animal, Custis. Wherever Mad Dog went, he'll definitely be remembered."

Longarm finished his drink. "Maybe I'll go over to the Bulldog and have another talk with Brice."

Tony blinked. "You mean you've already talked to him?"

"Yes."

"And he didn't mention knowing and managing Mad Dog?"

"Nope."

"You be real careful over there, Marshal. I know you can take care of yourself but that's a murderous bunch at the Bulldog. You'd better be on your toes if you start asking the wrong kind of questions in that saloon."

"Thanks for the information and warning," Longarm said, reaching for his money to pay for the drinks.

"It's on the house," Tony said. "And don't worry, I won't say a thing about those names, all of which I've already forgotten except for Mad Dog Trabert and Jude. Want me to ask my bartender and some of my people if they've heard of Jude?"

"Sure. Just don't tell them who's interested."

"Gotcha!"

They stood up and shook hands. Tony flashed the finest, whitest set of teeth in town and patted Longarm on

36

the shoulder. "You take care at the Bulldog, Marshal."

"I will."

"Who should I contact if I hear anything about a man named Jude?"

"Me or my boss, Billy Vail."

"I know Billy. He used to be a regular years ago before he became a happily married man. He's a good guy and you can tell him I said hello."

"I will, Tony."

Longarm left and headed back to the Bulldog. He had planned to do so tomorrow but now that he had a connection between Brice and Mad Dog Trabert, he knew that he couldn't stand the suspense of waiting to get his answers. It would mean that he'd be late again getting to see Polly, but the woman knew the responsibility he'd shouldered and she'd understand.

Chapter 5

Longarm could hardly keep from breaking into a trot as he hurried across town to revisit the Bulldog Saloon. He would confront Brice and ask him about Mad Dog Trabert, and the man had better not try any double-talk or Longarm would pressure him hard, even threaten to get his saloon closed down.

It was nearly dark when he stepped into the Bulldog; the contrast between it and Tony's Place couldn't have been more pronounced. There was a stench here and, unless you had tossed down a half dozen beers or whiskeys, it was almost enough to gag a man.

The saloon was packed and as soon as Longarm was recognized, the conversation was replaced by sullen and even openly hostile glares.

"What the hell are you doing back here?" Brice demanded when he saw that his customers had stopped drinking.

"We need to talk."

"I got nothing more to tell you. Now get out of here! You make my customers uneasy."

Longarm's eyes raked the crowd and he spotted a familiar face. "Hello, Horace," he said. "I didn't know that they'd let you out of prison so soon."

Horace Climer had mugged and robbed a grocery clerk and left him lying on the boardwalk with a cracked skull. Now, he stared at Longarm and growled, "I wouldn't have been there at all if it hadn't been for you, Marshal."

"Horace, I'm betting you won't be free more than six months. Maybe next time you'll get what you really deserve . . . a hangman's noose."

The burly mugger's face twisted with hatred. "You'll get what's comin' to you one of these days."

"Maybe," Longarm said, "but when I do you'll already be rotting in a pauper's grave."

Brice shouldered his way through the hostile crowd and stopped in front of Longarm. "Get out of here," he demanded.

"Not until we talk."

Brice rushed past Longarm and waddled out into the street. Whirling around with a dirty bar towel clenched in his round fist, he said, "Dammit, Marshal, you've no right to come into my place and raise hell with my customers!"

"I didn't 'raise hell' with anybody. I just asked to speak to you and you refused so I decided to talk to an old enemy." Longarm shot a glance back toward the saloon. "That man nearly murdered his victim and he should have gotten at least ten years in prison."

"Yeah, well maybe so. But you have no idea how close you just came to being jumped in there and beaten to a pulp."

Longarm wasn't interested in what Brice had to say about what could have happened to him inside. He turned his attention back to Brice and said, "I want you to tell me everything that you know about Mad Dog Trabert."

Brice stared. "Who?"

"Mad Dog Trabert. The brawler from New York that you staked and managed about five years ago. And don't

40

tell me that you don't remember the man or else I promise you that this conversation will continue down at the main jail."

Brice swallowed hard and although the night air was cool, he began to sweat and had to mop his round face with his bar rag. "All right. I knew him. So what?"

"Where is Mad Dog right now?"

"How the hell should I know! He killed a man in a fight and came lookin' for my help. I told him to beat it out of Denver before he got lynched. That's the last I saw of him."

"Are you absolutely sure?"

"Of course!"

"Where did he go?"

"I don't know!"

Longarm grabbed Brice and shoved him hard into the wall of his own building. "I haven't got time to play games. You must know where he went and I expect you to tell me right now, or so help me, I'll drag your fat ass off to jail."

"The last I heard he went up to Central City!"

"The same place as Carl, huh?"

"I don't know. I guess. I didn't keep track of Mad Dog. He was nothing but trouble and he almost got me killed out in the back alley. I couldn't get rid of him fast enough."

"Have you seen or heard from him in the past five years?"

"Uh . . . no."

Longarm grabbed the fat man again and slammed him back against the building a second time. "You're lying!"

"All right. All right. He's come down from Central City a couple of times a year. He always asks me for money. He tries to get me to set him up with fights like before but I told him I wanted nothing to do with his craziness.

41

It's one thing to whip a man, another to beat him nearly to death."

Longarm released Brice and stepped back. "I don't know if you're telling me the whole truth or not . . . but you'd better be because I will find those two men. When I do, I'll ask them about how much contact they've had with you and their stories better match your story. Understand?"

Brice swallowed hard. "I got to go back inside. My bartender can't be trusted. He's probably pouring free whiskey to his friends and putting money in his own pocket. Please, I got to make a livin'!"

Longarm let the man go but yelled before he passed back inside, "I'll be in touch with you, Brice. You remember anything about that bank robbery, you'd better tell me!"

Brice slithered through the doorway without a backward glance. Longarm knew that he'd put a hell of a good scare into the saloon owner and he hoped that the man would take his threat seriously.

Longarm walked away thinking, *I'll go spend another night with Polly and then head over to see Billy Vail and tell him about this new information. After that, I ought to have enough time to catch the stage up to Central City and see if Carl and Mad Dog are still in town. With luck, at least one of them is still there and I'll get my first big break on this case.*

As Longarm approached Polly's apartment, he had a sense that something was amiss. Polly's windows were ablaze with light and the front curtains were drawn tightly.

He knocked on her door and called her name. The door flew open and Polly threw herself into his arms. "Custis, someone has been here today. They ransacked my apartment!"

"A thief?"

She drew him inside and closed then locked the door. Although Polly had things straightened up, Longarm could see that the couch and chairs had been slashed and all the drawers emptied, their contents strewn across the floor. Longarm picked up a porcelain figurine of a running horse. It had been beautiful and expensive, but now its head was broken off and it was worthless.

"Did you lose any jewelry or money?"

"Yes, but not a great deal. I keep my savings and the few pieces of good jewelry I own at the bank."

"There's been a rash of thefts lately."

"Custis, I'm not sure that this was just an ordinary theft."

"What do you mean?"

Polly shuddered. "The man who did this was waiting in here for me to open the door."

"How do you know that?"

"Because I had invited a couple of my friends from the office to come home with me to visit. My guess is that when the thief realized that I wasn't alone, instead of attacking me when I entered . . . he ran."

"Did you actually see him?"

"I heard his running footsteps as I was opening the door. Then, when I looked down the hallway, I saw him leap out my back bedroom window."

"Are you sure about that?"

Polly nodded. "I don't mind telling you that I'm really afraid. I think, if I'd been alone, he would have attacked me!"

"We don't know that for certain."

"But he was *waiting* for me. I mean, if he was just a thief, wouldn't he have left as soon as he'd found everything of value?"

"Maybe he was leaving when you appeared."

Polly took a deep breath. "I sure hope so, but I have my doubts."

"You're a beautiful young woman and it's not unrealistic to think that some man followed you home, then came back and broke into the apartment."

"What am I going to do?" Polly wrapped her arms around him. "Custis, I'm frightened."

"I'll stay the night, of course. In the morning, I'll get a good locksmith to reinforce your doors. We'll also have to do something about the windows front and back to prevent entry."

Polly turned her face up to him and asked, "Do you think it might have something to do with your investigation?"

"No, why . . ."

"I caught a glimpse of the man and he was tall and thin. And from the damage he did, it's obvious that he carried a large knife. Like a Bowie knife or something." She shuddered and rested her head against his chest. "He would have used that knife on me."

Longarm didn't want to unnecessarily alarm Polly, but he could feel a nagging dread building up inside that this actually might have been the work of the knife fighter, Carl Appleby. And, if that was even the remotest of possibilities, he had to get Polly out of here until the man was apprehended or killed.

Polly studied his face. "Could this have had something to do with that bank robbery and your questioning people the past two days all over Denver?"

"I don't think so," he replied, "but let's not take any chances. You'd better live at my apartment until this business is over. I've fortified it so that no one could possibly break in and you'd be safe there until we are positive that you're not in danger."

"But why would anyone want to hurt me?"

"I don't know," he admitted. "But the men I am hunting have no morals. They've already demonstrated that they'll kill anybody."

"I'd better pack my clothes and belongings."

"Good idea."

Longarm picked up a few of the leftover odds and ends, his mind racing. Had Carl Appleby come by here to attack Polly? Or perhaps silence her and then wait in ambush for an unsuspecting Marshal Long to appear? That seemed like a farfetched notion until Longarm remembered what the floor of the bank had looked like right after eight innocent people had been executed.

Longarm paced the floor. Yes, he thought, it was best to play it safe and have Polly stay at his apartment until he tracked down Carl and Mad Dog. And if it was either of those people, they must have . . . talked to Brice at the Bulldog. Of course! Tony over at Tony's Place would never have spoken to that pair. So, if Carl Appleby or Mad Dog had been in this apartment, their source of information must have been Brice.

Longarm made the decision right then and there to go over to see the owner of the Bulldog Saloon the next morning. Brice would certainly deny having spoken to Carl or Mad Dog but Longarm thought he could detect a lie and, if he pressured the saloon owner hard enough, he was certain that Brice would crack.

The next morning, Longarm escorted a still-upset Polly from his apartment to the federal building, the stares of their co-workers and the gossip be damned. They kissed in the lobby with everyone watching and then Polly asked, "What are you going to do now?"

"I'm going to talk to someone who might know something about what happened last night at your apartment."

"Then you *do* think your investigation and that break-in are related!"

"That's a real possibility. Not a strong one but a possibility that I have to investigate before I'll feel safe about letting you return to your own apartment. And I'll also

45

contact that locksmith and have him upgrade your door locks and then put some bars over your outside windows."

"Like a jail?"

"You'll sleep better," Longarm assured the attractive young woman. "By the way, do you own a handgun?"

"No."

"I'm going to give you one and show you how to use it," he promised.

"I'm not sure that I could pull the trigger," she confessed.

"If that someone was about to rape or kill you," Longarm replied, "I'm confident that you'd shoot the man to save yourself. At least, I'd hope you would. There's nothing honorable about allowing yourself to be attacked without putting up a fight."

"I suppose not."

"Polly, I have an extra derringer back at the apartment. It isn't much for accuracy but, at close range, I promise you that it's a man stopper."

She kissed him again with everyone watching, and then Longarm went up to see Billy Vail and sound his boss out concerning the break-in that had just occurred at Polly's apartment. If Billy also believed there might be some connection between that crime and Longarm's investigation, then he would definitely rush over to the Bulldog and have a few hard words with Brice.

A few minutes later, sitting alone with Billy, Longarm told his boss about the previous day's and evening's events. As he talked, Billy became more and more grim-faced. And when Longarm was finished, Billy said, "I'm going with you to question Brice. I know that fat scum well enough to pull up a thing or two from his past that might convince him he'd better come clean."

"Then get your coat," Longarm drawled.

They headed on over to the Bulldog, Custis's long legs making Billy's short legs fly in order to match his rapid

46

pace. It was exactly nine o'clock when Longarm pounded on the front door of the closed-up Bulldog Saloon.

"Brice had always lived in an apartment attached to the back of this place," Billy remembered. "He's probably asleep there so let's have a look."

They walked around to the alley and located the apartment. When they knocked, there was no answer.

"Brice Papp, this is Marshal Billy Vail! I've got Deputy Marshal Custis Long with me and you had better open up this door and answer some gawdamn questions right now."

Still no response.

"He's in there," Billy snapped. "Kick the door open."

Longarm reared back and slammed it good and hard with the heel of his boot. Wood cracked in protest but the hinges stubbornly refused to break free.

"Kick it again," Billy ordered. "He's just hoping that we'll give up and go away."

Longarm kicked the door three more times before the hinges separated from the doorjamb and the door broke free.

"Come on out, Brice!" Billy shouted.

"Look," Longarm said, pointing down at the floor. "Either that's oil of some kind or . . . blood."

"Holy cow!" Billy cried, staring down at the dark stains on the floor. "It is blood!"

They rushed inside to find the saloon owner's naked, bloated body lying face up on the floor. Brice Papp hadn't just been stabbed, he'd been skewered and mutilated. His round, chubby face was a frozen mask of terror and a bar rag had been stuffed into his mouth making him look like a giant chipmunk. His nose had been hacked off and so had his ears. A deep, horrible X-shaped wound had been sliced across his massive, blubbery chest. The fatal wounds were probably the ones that had pierced his huge beer belly. Longarm counted six stab wounds and there was no doubt that they had been inflicted with a Bowie knife.

Billy turned his head away for a moment and then took a deep breath. The apartment was littered with rotting food and empty whiskey bottles. Billy whispered, "This looks like the floor of a slaughterhouse. I've got to get some fresh air."

Longarm had the same need. They both pushed back outside and took several mind-clearing gulps of breath. "Well," Longarm commented, "I don't think there's much doubt anymore about who did that."

"The one named Carl Appleby?"

"Yes. And now I'm certain that he did visit Polly's apartment yesterday."

"We'd better assign a man to protect her," Billy said. "Where is she?"

"She's going to spend her nights at my apartment."

"We can do better than that. No offense," Billy said, "but I've seen your apartment and although it isn't as bad as this one . . . it's no palace."

Longarm wasn't offended. He had never pretended to be a good housekeeper. "So where else can she stay?"

"At my house with my wife and family."

Longarm nodded. "All right."

"So you'll be hunting Carl Appleby today?"

"That's right."

"Any clue where to start?"

"I'm going to visit all the wagon freighters in Denver today. Brice told me that Carl was a muleskinner."

"I'll go with you."

"What about him?" Longarm asked, jerking his thumb back to the scene of the grisly murder.

"I'll send some people over to take care of the body and see if they can find anything of interest to us."

"You know," Billy said, "if we don't turn up a lead on

48

Carl, we might have to use you or Polly as bait to draw him out of hiding."

"I'm willing to act as a lure, but Polly is off limits," Longarm snapped.

"Why? He knows her apartment and he obviously thinks that you told her his name. My bet is that he'll try her apartment again in a day or two."

Longarm could see the logic. "If we come up short with the freight offices and have no leads whatsoever as to how and where to find the man, then I'll go hide in Polly's apartment."

"Well," Billy said, "let's just hope it don't come to that."

Longarm nodded with agreement and started up the alley trying to push the image of the mutilated saloon owner out of his mind. Brice Papp sure hadn't been a model citizen, but no one deserved to die in that kind of slow and horrible agony.

Chapter 6

Making the rounds of the Denver freighting companies was going to be a bit more pleasant than making the rounds of all the saloons. In the first place, there weren't nearly as many, and, in the second place, livestock barns and corrals actually smelled better than most seedy saloons.

"We're looking for a man named Carl Appleby," Billy said, after introducing himself and Longarm. "Does someone by that name work for you?"

"Nope" was the answer they kept getting.

At each place they visited, the answer continued to be no. But several of the people said they remembered a muleskinner who fitted Carl Appleby's description.

When that happened, Billy would give them his business card and ask that they contact his office if Carl, or whatever name he was now using, appeared seeking employment.

Together, Longarm and Billy Vail worked steadily through the morning, had a good midday meal at a cafe called the Yellow Jacket where they were served the best chili and corn bread in town, and then continued interviewing at the freighting offices.

51

By three o'clock in the afternoon, Billy was ready to call it a day. "I'll bet we've visited fifteen freighting companies so far and I'm not even sure if there are any others."

"There are," Longarm assured his boss. "What's the matter, are your feet or legs giving out?"

"Yeah, a little. But I'm not quitting if you're not," Billy assured him. "I'm just a little out of shape, that's all. This exercise is good for me."

"There are two or three more freighting companies about a half-mile beyond the train yards," Longarm told his exhausted friend. "It's not far enough to warrant renting a coach or a horse. Maybe you should return to the office."

"Hell no! I'm coming. Just . . . just slow down a little," Billy snapped, his face flushed from the effort of trying to keep up with his tall friend.

"Suit yourself, but I'd like to finish this up today rather than leave some for tomorrow morning."

"We'll finish," Billy said, "quit rushing me."

Longarm was anxious and angry about how close Polly had come to being carved up and murdered like Brice Papp. Just the thought of someone doing that turned his stomach in knots.

"There's the railroad depot," Longarm said, as they clomped along beside the tracks. "The daily run up to Cheyenne will be leaving shortly."

"Yeah," Billy said, stumbling over a large chunk of coal and then kicking another chunk aside in exasperation. "I used to travel up there regularly on cases."

"Do you miss it?"

"I do," Billy admitted. "Some days at the office fly past but most drag. I remember when I had your job every day flew by so fast. In fact, I recall that some months and even years flew by. But not anymore. My job isn't much fun. I'm not even sure that it's important."

"Of course it is."

"Thanks, but I often wonder if I earn my pay."

"Just surviving in that office arena is quite a chore," Longarm said. "I know I sure couldn't handle the politics and pressure, not to mention the paperwork."

"It's tedious and often difficult and not very rewarding," Billy admitted. "I mean, when the noose goes over a murderer's head, *you're* the one that brought him to justice. Saw him convicted and sentenced, and that's an accomplishment that can't be taken too lightly. You risked your life and you bested an outlaw that would have killed you . . . if you hadn't been the smarter, tougher man."

"What you say is true," Longarm agreed, "but you do things that are tough too."

"Not really. The paperwork to keep the machinery going so that we have the funds to send men like yourself out to do the real work is necessary and, therefore, I suppose important. But there's little satisfaction in it for me."

Longarm slowed down. "So what are you going to do, Billy? You've got a family to support, a big house to pay for and lots of bills."

"I don't quite know," Billy answered. "But sometimes I think of leaving the federal government and striking out on my own."

"Doing what?"

"That's the part I don't know yet. I'm too old and fat to work hard anymore . . . though I could toughen up again."

"Sure, but . . ."

"I've got a friend that loves being a gunsmith. He's got that shop on Larimer Street called, called Straight Shooters. I stop in and talk to him sometimes after a day at the office. I love guns, and sometimes, when my friend is overloaded with work, I'll spend a few hours on weekends helping him out. He says that I could learn to be a fine gunsmith and he'd be willing to teach me."

Longarm held his silence. He guessed that the gunsmith didn't earn half what Billy earned, even given his successful business. Longarm knew Billy's wife was a good and understanding woman but he doubted if she'd be very happy moving into a small house and pinching pennies.

"Anyway," Billy was saying, "I've been thinking some about going into business for myself. Maybe open a little feed store or saddle shop."

"You don't know anything about feed stores and you sure aren't a saddle maker."

"Yeah, I know. But I'm not so old that I couldn't start over and learn a new trade, Custis. I'm not a lazy man."

"Of course not. But you have a wife and children and that big house payment to make."

Billy kicked another lump of coal and they plodded along down the tracks and past the train depot. "I just don't want to spend my life sitting at a desk bored. Or listening to my employees tell me boring stories about very personal things I don't want to hear. You understand where I'm coming from, don't you?"

"I sure do."

"That's why I needed to come along with you today. To just get out of the office and away from the head of our agency. To be honest, Mr. Ludlow drives me crazy!"

"I never had much to do with him," Longarm said.

"Count yourself lucky. He would never have gotten his job if his wife hadn't been the daughter of our former United States senator. Did you know that?"

"Yep."

"It isn't that Walt Ludlow is a bad administrator or person," Billy said. "It's just that he doesn't *do* anything. He delegates everything to me or one of the other department heads. When we mess up, we get the blame, but when we do something really good, he takes the credit! Now I ask you, is that fair?"

"Not a bit fair."

"You bet it isn't. And the man is real gassy."

" 'Gassy?' "

"Yeah," Billy sighed. "He comes in my office and I swear you'd think something had died by the time he leaves. I have to open all the windows and light up a cigar. It's bad enough to kill flying insects."

"Huh. I never noticed that about Mr. Ludlow."

"If you were around him more than ten minutes you would. I've been cooped up in a small room for hours with him and I damn near turned green. I tell you, Custis, my job might look pretty cushy, but it has some major drawbacks."

"I can see that now." Longarm pointed up the tracks. "That's the Pioneer Freighting Company. The owner is named Elden Pierce. He's an ex-con."

"Really?" Billy asked, momentarily forgetting his miseries at the office. "How do you know that?"

"Because he was a former stagecoach robber who worked mostly in New Mexico. He's the kind that would hire a man as hard as himself. Someone like Carl Appleby."

"Since you know him, do you want to do the talking this time?"

"Sure," Longarm agreed.

Longarm knew that Pioneer Freight operated supply wagons up into the Rocky Mountains, and, from what he could see, they were a fair-sized outfit now. There were two huge corrals, one filled with horses, the other with mules. A big wagon barn held maybe a half-dozen freight wagons in various stages of repair; there was also a house, a tool shed, another barn stacked with hay, and what appeared to be a combination blacksmith and harness shop. As they approached the freight company, Longarm grew more alert. After all, it was possible that the knife fighter could be working here today and Carl would recognize him on sight.

"They're a pretty big operation," Billy said. "The guy might be an ex-con, but he's done all right."

"I'd say so. I haven't been here in maybe six or seven years. Back then, you could have bought Elden Pierce and everything he owned for ten dollars. I'm surprised he's done so well."

"Do you think he'll be honest with us?"

"I do," Longarm replied. "Not because he's a good citizen . . . because he isn't. Elden would rob his own mother. But the thing is, he didn't take well to prison and I know he'd do anything to stay free."

"Most men would."

"Yeah," Longarm agreed, "but I heard that Elden Pierce nearly went crazy behind bars. When you meet the man, look deep into his eyes and you'll see what I mean."

"I will."

"That's him," Longarm said when a short but powerful-looking man dressed in bib overalls and wearing a straw hat stepped out of the house and stood waiting for them to arrive.

"He looks kind of tough," Billy said.

"He is. Just let me handle this. Okay?"

"Sure. But if I think he's lying to us and knows where our killer is . . . then I'm going to speak up."

"Okay."

Longarm lifted his hand in greeting but Pierce didn't respond. When they stopped in front of his combination office and house, two big dogs the size of wolves crawled out from under the front porch, ruffs standing up and growling. The animals were so mean-looking that Longarm warned, "Elden, if they try to bite us, I'll draw my gun and shoot them both."

The man swore at his guard dogs and they retreated back under the porch growling. Pierce had a sneer on his brutish face when he asked, "What can I do for you today, Marshal?"

56

"We're looking for a muleskinner."

"There's a few around here working for me. Some of 'em are out on the road. Are you looking for any particular muleskinner?"

"Yeah," Longarm said. "One named Carl Appleby."

Pierce glanced to one side, then back to Longarm and said, "The name don't ring a bell with me, Marshal. Who is your little sidekick?"

"My name is Marshal Bill Vail," Billy snapped, obviously miffed at the reference. "And, if you're lying about not knowing Carl Appleby, you'll find out real fast who I am. So you'd better be telling the truth, Mr. Pierce, or you'll wind up back in prison."

Pierce's eyes hardened. "You lawmen are all alike . . . always using that badge to push people around. I'm an honest businessman now. I've gone straight and made a big success of myself!"

Longarm took a good look in the direction this man had glanced but he didn't see anyone. There were, however, a few employees that could be seen working on wagons and in the blacksmith and tool shops.

"Mind if we look around?" Longarm asked.

"Yeah, as a matter of fact I do mind. But then, you'd do it anyway, right?"

"That's right."

"Then help yourself. Just don't steal anything, boys!" Elden Pierce thought that was funny. He chuckled and folded his arms across his barrel chest. "If I thought you were stealing from me, then I'd have to call the *law*."

He laughed but Longarm didn't give him the satisfaction of seeing his anger; instead he turned and headed off toward the work sheds and barns, hand near his six-gun just in case Carl was hiding in the shadows with a Bowie knife clenched in one hand and a six-gun in the other.

Longarm strode across the big freight yard, and when he came to the toolshed and blacksmith shop, he found himself facing two shirtless smithies with hammers clenched in their sweaty fists.

"Afternoon," he said, not bothering to give the pair a smile. "Is there anyone else working in here?"

They didn't answer but did finally decide to shake their heads back and forth.

"Not that I doubt your word," Longarm said, "but I'm going to have to look inside."

The larger of the pair, a muscular young man with a red beard and menacing stare, blocked Longarm's path, hammer tapping his leather apron.

"Bert, let him look around!" Pierce shouted. "He won't find what he's after!"

Bert was slow about moving but Longarm didn't push the young man. That hammer in his fist was a mean-looking weapon. Longarm went into the shed and checked it out carefully. He saw plenty of busted wagon wheels and other pieces of equipment in need of repair, but Carl wasn't in there hiding.

"Go on about your work," Longarm said, heading for the barns with Billy in tow.

"Damn, this is a hostile place!" Billy swore. "These people just plain don't like the law."

"It all comes down from the top," Longarm replied. "Elden Pierce hates all lawmen with an abiding passion. He attracts the same kind, and I'll just bet every one of them has either been in prison . . . or is heading for prison. That's why this is such a likely place for a muleskinner like Carl Appleby to work."

Carl wasn't hiding in the hay barn either. When Longarm entered the wagon repair barn, it was so dark inside that he paused a few minutes to let his eyes adjust.

"Just watch my back and I'll do the same for you," he told Billy. "If our killer is in here, he's got a lot of places to hide."

"You're right," Billy said, hand on his own sidearm.

"He could be in any one of these wagons."

"We'd better check them all," Longarm decided. "It's going to be dirty, dangerous work but I think we have to do it anyway."

"I agree. If I were hiding from the law, this is where I'd have run when we appeared coming up the railroad tracks."

Longarm drew his six-gun and Billy did the same. "Stay close and we'll work through these wagons and all this junk together."

"Sounds good," Billy whispered, unable to hide his excitement. "Damned if I don't feel the old juices starting to flow again after all these years."

Longarm couldn't resist a smile. He was glad that Billy was feeling so alive again . . . he just wanted to make sure they stayed that way. "We'll start over here on the right and work to the end of the barn. You look under the wagons; I'm taller so I'll look inside them."

"Sounds right to me."

Longarm began to move down through the dusty barn as quiet as possible. Each time he came to a big, ruined freight wagon, he'd have to stand on his toes and peer over the back into its bed. Sometimes, he saw piles of canvas or old tarps and he had to pull them out and make sure that no one was hiding under them. It was a dirty job and he knew that his clothes would soon be filthy.

"It's hot in here and there's no moving air," Billy said, climbing back to his feet after looking under the wagon and moving some old water barrels. "I'm sweating like a pig."

"Me too," Longarm said. "Just try not to talk. If he's in here, we don't want him to know where we are unless he sticks his head up and risks being seen."

"Yeah, right. Sorry."

"No problem," Longarm said in a low voice.

They inspected every wagon on the right side of the

barn and started down the left side. A bat in the rafters suddenly burst into flight and startled Billy so badly that he drew his gun and fired in one not-so-swift and fairly clumsy movement. His bullet knocked a little hole in the roof and created a thin shaft of dusty light.

Elden and several of his men came running. "What the hell is going on in here?"

"Nothing," Longarm said. "Go back to your own business."

"This barn and having a good roof on it is my business," Pierce retorted. "Gawdammit, there's no one hiding in here!"

"We'll decide that for ourselves," Longarm said. "Now git!".

Elden Pierce hesitated. "Look," he said. "You're wasting your time and mine. Why . . ."

"We'll be done soon," Longarm told the man.

"Yeah, well this ain't right, you guys comin' in here and going over my place with a fine-toothed comb like this. As you can see, this barn ain't locked up and sometimes . . . ah, never mind."

Longarm twisted around. "What were you going to tell me, Elden?"

"Nothing!"

The man turned on his heel and hurried away. Longarm said, "Billy, wouldn't you say that Mr. Pierce is a tad nervous?"

"Yeah," Billy whispered. "A lot more nervous than he should be."

Longarm took a deep breath, drew his gun and started forward, peering into wagons. "That's what I'm thinking too."

They were almost to the end of the barn when it happened. One moment Longarm was up on his toes looking into the bed of a rickety freight wagon and the next he heard a strangled cry.

Whirling around, he saw the silhouette of a man leaping up from under a rotting tarp and tackling Billy. Longarm saw the man raise his arm and bring it down with a knife in his fist.

Longarm fired without thinking, and his bullet must have struck the man somewhere because he fell away from Billy. Longarm fired again, but the shadowy figure was diving under the wagons and racing off into the darkness.

"Billy!" The deskbound marshal was covered with blood. "Billy, talk to me!"

"I'm stuck," Billy said weakly as he struggled to get up. "He stuck me pretty good, Custis. Go after him."

"I'm going to get you to a doctor."

"Custis," Billy weakly protested, "if you don't go after him, he's going to get away!"

Longarm scooped him up in his arms and carried him outside into the bright afternoon sunlight. Billy had a deep stab wound under his left armpit and was losing far too much blood.

"Pierce," Longarm shouted, "get a wagon over here quick!"

The freight company owner ran up and stared at Billy. "Is he dying?"

"He will if I don't get him to a doctor." Longarm's mouth twisted in fury. "And if he dies, by damned I'll see that you're sent back to prison for life without parole!"

"But . . . but I didn't know anyone was in there!"

"Get a wagon!"

Pierce didn't need any more urging. Fortunately, there happened to be a buckboard already hitched to a pair of horses. It was loaded with grain but there was room for Billy and Longarm. Custis used his pocket knife to rip into a grain sack for bandaging. Holding the bandage tight against Billy's shoulder, he yelled, "Let's go!"

Pierce sent the horses racing for town and when they

arrived, Billy was still conscious but pale and breathing fast.

"Stop at Dr. Carter's office just up the street!" Longarm bellowed.

"Is he still alive?" Pierce yelled from the driver's seat.

"Barely. You got some hard questions to answer."

"He told me his name was Bill Sheldon!" Pierce cried. "Marshal, I didn't know he was the man you were looking for. I swear I didn't!"

Longarm leaned over close to his boss. "Just hang on. Dr. Carter will get you fixed up."

"I hope so." Billy gazed up at Longarm. "But, if I don't make it, keep after them, Custis. Don't let them get away again."

"You're going to make it. Just hang on and fight."

The moment the buckboard came to a stop, Longarm was jumping to the ground. He eased Billy out of the wagon and shouted, "Open the door and call for the doc!"

"Sure thing."

Dr. Gideon Carter was nearing retirement age. He was short-tempered and abrupt with his patients but steady and competent.

When Carter saw all the blood pouring out of Billy, he had them lay him on a table. "He was knifed?"

"Yeah."

The doctor quickly removed Billy's coat, vest and finally his blood-soaked shirt. Adjusting his spectacles, he said, "You boys roll him over on his side so I can see if he's still got a chance."

Longarm and Elden Pierce did as they were ordered. Carter pitched the bloody bandaging aside and studied the wound very carefully. By now, Billy was really getting pale and shaky.

"He's been stuck hard but maybe not too deep," Carter said, finger pressing down on the leaking hole in Billy's side. "A thin knife would have passed between the ribs,

62

but a Bowie is so thick and heavy a blade that it has to cut through the ribs. This one didn't do that. From all the tissue damage, it looks to me like the knife hit this man a glancing blow."

Longarm grabbed Billy's shoulder. "You hear that? The doc says that the blade didn't go deep."

Billy's eyelids fluttered. "I feel like I've been skewered like a pig on a roasting pole."

"What's a man in your age and condition doing in a knife fight?" Carter demanded.

Longarm told Carter that Billy was a federal marshal and that he had been jumped by surprise and stabbed in a wagon barn.

"You're probably going to live," Carter finally announced. "All I can do is stitch you up and keep you from losing any more blood. The rest is up to you."

Longarm stayed a few more minutes before Carter ordered him and Elden Pierce out of the room. "You men wait outside and I'll talk to you when I'm finished. And I'll want to be paid ten dollars."

When they went outside, the first thing that Longarm did was to drive his fist into Elden Pierce's face. The freight company owner crashed into the wheel of his wagon, lips crushed like grapes. He spat a tooth and cried, "Why'd you do that?"

"Because you knew a man was hiding in you barn! And you knew he'd use his knife!"

"No, I didn't."

Longarm was so furious he waded into Pierce, swinging from all angles and beating the man nearly to a pulp. When Pierce couldn't speak because of the blood he was spitting up, Longarm dragged him over to a public horse-watering trough and shoved his head under water. He held Pierce under until the man began to thrash wildly, then he let him up for air and hurled him to the earth.

Longarm knelt on the man's heaving chest, grabbed his

side whiskers, and said, "I'm going to beat you to death right now unless you tell me where that man went after he left your barn."

"I . . . I don't know!"

Longarm balled his fist and drew it back. Pierce screeched and tried to protect his face from further destruction. "All right! He was running for the train! That's all I know! He's off to Cheyenne!"

Longarm heard the train's mighty steam whistle blow.

"Get in to the doctor and when he's finished with Billy, have him fix your damned ugly face!" Longarm shouted as he raced toward a horse tied at a nearby hitching rail. "And you'd better pay for the both of you!"

The train was leaving. Billy was in the doctor's hands and there was nothing more that Longarm could do to help his friend. Nothing, that is, except overtake that northbound train and capture or, better yet, kill Carl Appleby.

Chapter 7

Longarm untied the horse and was just about to mount up when a cowboy stormed out of a nearby saloon, drew his gun and shouted, "Put your damned foot in that stirrup and I'll blow a hole in you big enough for a crow to fly though, Mister!"

"I'm a United States marshal and I have to catch that train!"

"Then find your own damned horse but you ain't takin' mine."

Longarm could tell by the look on the cowboy's face that no amount of argument was going to change his mind. So he glanced up and down the street and saw the nearest horse was about a hundred yards away. There was nothing to do but run, and he was pretty winded by the time he untied it and swung into the saddle. He reined the horse around and rode up the street.

"You'll hang for stealin' that fella's horse!" the cowboy yelled.

Longarm paid the man no attention. Because of the city buildings, he couldn't see the train leaving the station, but he could see puffs of smoke from its stack and they were moving steadily north. Longarm had barely glanced at the horse he'd taken but now he realized it was a strawberry roan, slow, fat and probably old.

"Dammit, anyway," he swore. Since he wasn't wearing spurs and had no quirt, he was having a tough time even making the animal gallop because it insisted on trotting. "Ya!"

After a teeth-shattering trot up the street, he yanked off his hat and used it to fan the roan's behind, forcing it to break into a lumbering gallop. When he finally cleared the buildings, he could see that the train was a half mile away and gathering speed.

Longarm was booting the roan in the ribs and fanning its backside with all his might and gradually narrowing the gap. "Come on!" he shouted, working nearly as hard as the roan. "You can do it!"

The roan laid back its ears, lowered its head and ran for all it was worth until Longarm was nearly even with the train's caboose. The trouble was he'd been galloping below the track's slightly elevated bed, but now he had to rein the winded horse up onto the cinders so that he could get within reach of the caboose. On a good horse with decent speed, it wouldn't have been a problem, but the animal stubbornly refused to move closer to the train. Somehow, his will prevailed and then they were up on the track bed, but the roan was starting to falter as its hooves crashed down on the railroad ties and each of its labored strides became shorter and choppier.

"Ya!" Longarm shouted, furiously beating the animal and leaning forward.

Another six feet and he'd make a jump for the railing of the caboose. It wouldn't be an impossible task. Now another three feet. Longarm stood up in the stirrups and bellowed at his mount. He reached out for the back rail of the caboose and just as he was about to throw himself out of the saddle in a desperate attempt to grab the railing, the roan stumbled. The next thing that Longarm knew, he was flying through the air. He caught a split-second glimpse of a shining rail coming up fast and then nothing but darkness.

"Marshal Long!" Dr. Carter was calling from a great distance. "Can you hear me? Wake up."

Longarm didn't want to wake up. His head felt as if it had been split in half by a wedge. When the doctor's shouting finally forced him to open his eyes, he had trouble focusing. There seemed to be *two* Dr. Carters leaning over him and they both looked damned worried.

"Marshal, can you see me?"

"Yeah, both of you."

"You've had a bad, bad spill. You've a concussion and maybe even some brain damage."

Longarm closed his eyes for a moment and tried to put some thoughts into a coherent order. Finally, memory began to return and he attempted to sit up, but the effort sent a jarring pain through his head.

"Easy," Dr. Carter warned, holding him down.

Longarm felt sick to his stomach and his head began to spin. "How is Billy?"

"He's going to be all right. I'm far more worried about your head than I am about his stab wound. Open your eyes wider."

Longarm did as he was told.

"Now," Carter said, "how many fingers am I holding up before you?"

"Four."

"Two," Carter corrected.

Longarm closed one eye and nodded. "Yeah, two."

"You really had a nasty crack on the head and you're lucky you weren't killed."

"I need to speak to Billy Vail."

"You will. That horse you took is all banged up and its owner wanted fifty dollars restitution. Not only for the

67

horse, but the saddle's stirrup must have gotten hooked onto a rail or spike because, when the animal struggled to its feet, it tore the saddle apart."

"That saddle and horse together weren't worth ten dollars!"

"Well," Carter said, "the man that owned him was so incensed that I took the money out of your pocket and just paid him all you had left. It came to a bit less than fifty but the man agreed to accept the lesser sum rather than raise any more of a stink."

"Let me talk to Billy."

"He's sleeping."

"He'd want to be awakened, Doc. So just do as I say and don't argue with me!"

Longarm grimaced because his outburst caused a burning needle to pierce his brain.

"All right," the doctor agreed. "But you're every bit as stubborn and foolish as Billy. That must be a common quality among United States marshals that I wasn't aware of."

Longarm closed his eyes. If only he'd have grabbed a good, fast horse! If he had, he'd have been able to leap onto the back railing of that train and, by now, he'd have either killed or apprehended Carl Appleby.

"Custis?"

Longarm opened his eyes to see Billy leaning over him. "Billy, Appleby escaped on the train. What time is it?"

"About six o'clock."

Longarm tried to concentrate and think. "The northbound wouldn't have arrived in Cheyenne yet. We could send a telegram with Appleby's description to the marshal up in Cheyenne. He could arrest our man when he got off the train."

"Good idea." He turned to Dr. Carter. "We need to send a telegram up to Cheyenne right now."

"You boys are sure demanding," Carter complained.

"You come in here and want to take things over."

"Doc," Billy said, "the man who stuck me and who helped rob our bank five years ago and execute all those innocent people is on that northbound train. We have to catch him or he'll get away and we'll never get the rest of that gang. Now, will you please just take a telegram and run it over to the telegraph office?"

"All right," Carter agreed. "Let me get a pencil and you can tell me what to write."

Longarm and Billy dictated a short telegram that gave the marshal of Cheyenne, a very capable lawman named Ruben Warner, a description of Carl Appleby. They added that Appleby was extremely dangerous and that Warner should be very careful when he made his arrest. Furthermore, Warner should take no chances with his prisoner, holding him until either Longarm or Billy could arrive to take custody.

"That ought to do it," Longarm said. "Let's just hope that Ruben gets the message before the train arrives."

"It's our only hope. If Ruben doesn't nab him, he may disappear forever. He could take a train either east or westbound."

"Doc," Billy said, "if you wouldn't mind putting a little speed on this, we'd appreciate it."

"Sure, why not?" Carter said, voice dripping with sarcasm. "You've both been giving me orders since you got here . . . why should I object to being a mere messenger boy now?"

"Thanks, Doc."

When Carter was gone, Longarm forced himself into a sitting position. He reached up and removed a bulky, turban-like bandage around his head. "Billy, if you find my hat, I'm getting out of here."

"In the first place, I have no idea where your hat is and, in the second place, you're not going anyplace without Dr. Carter's permission."

69

Longarm swung his legs off the table and the world revolved in a big, loopy circle. He gripped the edge of the table with all his might and the world gradually slowed. "You know that I have to get up to Cheyenne. Carl Appleby is the key. If we can take him alive, we finally have someone who will tell us where we can find the other gang members. And who Jude might be."

"I understand that, but I'll go. You stay here and recuperate."

"Not a chance." Longarm placed his stocking feet on the floor. "Where are my damned boots?"

"I'll get them for you."

Billy found his boots and gun belt. "For comfort, we'll rent a surrey and drive up to Cheyenne tonight. We can be there by morning and take Appleby into custody."

"Providing," Longarm said, "Ruben received our telegram or wasn't killed trying to arrest Appleby."

Billy nodded. "If he was killed, I'll take full responsibility."

"Ruben is a professional. We gave him a good description and a warning. Now, it's up to him to do the job. If he is killed, it's because he either ignored our warning, or he got careless. Either way, it's not your fault."

"Maybe not, but we should have got Appleby in the barn when we had him cornered. I let him stab me and you let the train get away so here we are all bunged up and holding an empty bag. Mistake after mistake and now Marshal Warner has to put his life on the line because of those mistakes."

"Let's get out of here," Longarm said, standing but feeling the room began to spin. "Grab my arm and give me a hand out the door."

"You're not fit to go walk across the street, much less get to Cheyenne."

"Neither are you," Longarm growled. "My head spins and you've lost a bucket of blood. But maybe, between

70

the two of us, we can just manage to do our jobs. You got any money to rent a surrey and a fast pair of horses? The doctor took every last cent in my wallet."

"No. I'd have to go back to the office and put in a voucher."

"Forget that," Longarm said. "By the time you got the government's money, it would be too late. Besides, we'd have to tell Mr. Ludlow the story and that would create a whole new set of problems. Right?"

"Right."

"If you haven't got enough, then we'll have to wait until Dr. Carter returns and borrow some more cash from him. He's such a skinflint that I'm sure he's got coffee cans of cash stashed all over this place."

Billy reached for his wallet and Longarm sure hoped they didn't have to wait for Dr. Carter. The man was crotchety and obstinate. Trying to pry a hundred dollars out of him would be like squeezing blood out of a stone.

Ten hours later, Longarm decided that he had probably felt worse in his life, but he really couldn't remember when. Now, morning dawned on the eastern horizon, soft and rosy-colored as the inside of a watermelon. His head still ached but at least he'd lost his troubling double vision. He and Billy had been forced to borrow money from Dr. Carter, promising to pay it back with ten dollars interest. That had really galled Longarm, but he'd put it behind him and tried to concentrate on what awaited them in Cheyenne. He sure hoped that Marshal Warner had gotten the telegraph in time and had been waiting for the train when an unsuspecting Carl Appleby disembarked.

"There's the train depot," Billy said, consulting his pocket watch. "It's only a little after six o'clock so Marshal Warner won't be in his office for at least another couple of hours."

71

"He might be if he arrested our man last evening on the train."

"Yeah, but why don't we stop at the train depot and ask if there was an arrest?"

"Make sense to me," Longarm replied.

When they drove up to the train depot, it was empty because there was no train due to arrive or depart for several hours. The telegraph office was located at the train depot. Furthermore, there was a telegraph operator on duty twenty-four hours a day. So they climbed down from the front seat of their rented surrey all stiff-legged and bent over like clothespins, and then both hobbled up the wide wooden stairs across the train platform and into the telegraph office. If was empty except for the operator, a man that Longarm knew and whose services he had used before.

"Howdy, Earl," he said.

Earl was a small, bespectacled man who reminded everyone of a disgruntled elf. He had large, protruding ears, a thatch of gray hair and a bobbing adam's apple. He was always rumpled, tired and out of sorts. Longarm knew that Earl had a heart condition and ought to have retired to a rocking chair, but he still had several children to clothe and feed and a chronic gambling habit that took more than a little of his meager paycheck.

"Marshal Long!" the little man cried, jumping up from his desk and rushing across the room. "Am I glad to see you!"

"Did you get the telegram delivered to Marshal Warner?"

"No. He quit his job last week and they still don't have a replacement."

Longarm's jaw nearly dropped. "Ruben Warner quit?"

Earl's head bobbed up and down. "He got in a big argument with the mayor and town council. They wouldn't give him a raise and so he accepted the marshal's job over in Laramie. Everyone is upset because he was . . ."

"What about the man we wanted apprehended?" Billy cried. "Did he just walk away?"

"Yes, but I recognized him getting off the train and . . ." Earl swelled up like a toad. "Marshal, I *tailed* him for you!"

"To where?"

"Is there a reward on his head that I could get?" Earl asked.

"No," Longarm said, reaching for his wallet. "But I've got ten dollars to pay you for your trouble."

"That isn't much to pay a family man for risking his life and his job," Earl wheedled. "After all, I left my desk and risked being fired, if not shot. I figured it was worth a whole lot more than ten dollars. What about your friend?"

"Billy," Longarm said, "you ought to kick in ten dollars too."

"What?" Billy was in no mood to be stiffed, but when he saw Longarm handing over cash, he must have realized that it was the smart thing to do. "Oh, here!" he snapped, matching Longarm's contribution.

Earl counted the money, arranged it neatly then stuffed it into his vest pocket saying, "I was hoping for a big reward. You sure that there's none being offered?"

"Afraid not," Longarm said, struggling for patience. "Now, Earl, where did our man go?"

"The Antelope Hotel," Earl said, eyes darting back and forth between them. "Room seven upstairs and facing main street. When I went home last night, I saw that he was still in there because there was a light shining through his window. Did I do good, Marshal Long?"

"You did great," Longarm said. "Just keep this news to yourself."

"I understand you, Marshal. You know, if I was young

and free, I'd be one hell of a fine lawman."

Longarm dipped his chin in agreement even though Earl was so puny that he would never have withstood the rigors of the profession. "You proved that," he said, following Billy out the door.

"Dammit," Billy said stormily, "isn't there anyone left who wants to do a good deed, not for personal gain, but simply out of the goodness of their hearts!"

"Earl is a good man but a bad gambler. Let's drive over to the Antelope Hotel and arrest Appleby. And stop grousing. That was the best ten dollars either of us ever spent."

"It will be if his information is correct and if Carl Appleby is still in that hotel room. But, if not, I'm coming back here to shake my ten dollars out of Earl's mercenary little hide!"

They climbed back into the wagon and Billy drove up the nearly empty main street toward the Antelope Hotel. A few saloons had stayed open all night and they saw several cowboys lying in a drunken stupor on the sidewalks. Several more were drinking from bottles on the front steps and they waved at Billy and Longarm as they passed.

"If Ruben was still marshal they wouldn't be hanging around like that," Longarm said. "He kept the streets and sidewalks of Cheyenne free of drunks. The mayor and town council will pay hell trying to find his replacement."

Billy had no comment. His face was pinched and pale, reminding Longarm how much blood he'd lost and how hard this trip had also been for him during the long, cold night they'd just spent.

"Billy," he said, "when we get up to room seven, you let me go in first."

"Not a chance. Your head is cracked and you'd miss your first shot and then I'd feel responsible for your death. I may be weak but there's nothing wrong with my aim. I'll go in first."

74

"No," Longarm insisted. "*I'll* go in first. You're too wide and slow a target."

Billy blanched. "Are you saying . . ."

"I'm saying that I'm the better man for this particular job. Now don't argue with me anymore! Arguing makes my head ache even worse."

"You're a damned difficult man, Custis. Damned difficult."

"And so are you."

They said nothing more and tied the team up about five buildings south of the Antelope Hotel. Longarm glanced up the street at the second story windows. They were all closed and curtained. He checked his gun and climbed down slowly from the wagon. "All right, Billy, the time for talk is over. Here we go."

Billy checked his own Colt. He started to carry it in his fist but Longarm said, "Why don't you put it back into your holster? No sense in alarming the hotel clerk or anyone else who sees us going up there. We'll *have* to take Carl Appleby alive. Otherwise, our murder investigation hits another dead end."

"Yeah," Billy agreed, holstering his gun. "You're right. But are you still seeing double?"

"No."

"Okay, then. You go in first and I'll follow."

"Why don't you stay down here in the street just in case Appleby tries to jump out his window."

"That's a pretty hard fall. Do you think he'd really do that?"

"Knowing that he'll hang in Denver he would," Longarm said. "Anyway, why take the chance? If he tries it, get the drop on him and make your arrest."

"But what if he . . ."

"I'll be all right," Longarm assured his friend. "I can take this man."

Billy finally nodded in reluctant agreement.

When Longarm entered the hotel lobby, the desk clerk was sound asleep, face lying on his hands. He was snoring loudly and a bottle of whiskey and an old newspaper were lying beside him. Longarm walked silently up to the hotel register and glanced at the names of the most recent guests. Carl Appleby's name wasn't recorded but that was expected. The man would be using an alias and, most likely, he'd only be staying in Cheyenne long enough to catch the next train out of town.

Not seeing any reason to rob the desk clerk of his sleep, Longarm tiptoed up the stairs and then entered the dim, narrow little hallway. He could feel his heart pounding and had to light a match in order to read the room numbers. When he came to number seven, he drew his six-gun. Knowing he had to be clearheaded when he went inside or else he'd soon be a dead man, Longarm deeply inhaled and exhaled several times.

He tried turning the doorknob just to make sure that it was locked as expected. Then, backing away and lowering his shoulder, Longarm drew his gun and threw himself at the door. It almost opened but almost wasn't good enough. Longarm stepped back and it was just his good fortune to do so because two bullets stitched through the wood and narrowly missed him.

"Appleby, this is Marshal Long. Drop your gun and come out with your hands over your head. You're under arrest!"

Appleby's reply came in the form of two more bullets. This time, Longarm was standing well aside of the door. He raised his own gun and fired back yelling, "You can't escape! Come out, or by gawd I'll kill you!"

There was no answer but the next thing Longarm heard was the sound of breaking glass. Longarm slammed into the door again just in time to see the fugitive disappear through the window. He heard a single gunshot from the street below, and by the time he got to the shattered window and peered out, he saw Billy standing over their man with his gun in his fist.

"Did you kill him?"

Billy looked up and shook his head. "He landed real hard and when he tried to raise his gun, I shot it out of his hand! Can you imagine! I fired without even aiming just like in the good old days. Then I pistol-whipped him. Carl Appleby isn't going to give us any more trouble for quite a while."

"Nice going!"

"Custis, are you all right?"

"Yeah," Longarm replied, steadying himself in the window frame. "A little dizzy but I'll be fine."

"Come on down and let's get him in the wagon and get out of here," Billy said.

"Be right there."

Longarm was a bit unsteady and navigated the stairs very carefully. The desk clerk, roused by all the shooting, was taking another pull on his bottle, and when he saw Longarm, he shoved it out of sight acting like a kid with his hand caught in his mother's cookie jar.

"Who are you?" he asked.

"Marshal Custis Long. Your guest in room seven just checked out."

"Uh . . . he did?"

"That's right." Longarm moved past him and out the front door. Several sleepy-looking people had already gathered to stare at Billy and his captive.

Billy was feeling good and in charge. "Custis, watch over him and I'll drive the wagon over here and we'll get some people to help us load him up."

Longarm nodded, as that seemed like a fine plan. And, in a very few minutes, they had Carl Appleby bound hand and foot and loaded into the backseat of their surrey.

"Who the hell are you men?" challenged a handsome,

77

well-dressed man who probably owned a successful business.

"I'm Deputy Marshal Long and this is my boss, Marshal Bill Vail," Longarm explained, fighting back a wave of dizziness.

"I insist upon some verification of that."

"What?" Longarm managed to ask.

"I insist upon seeing your badges right now!"

Longarm found his badge and showed it to the man who pointed at Billy and said, "Now I demand to see his badge."

Billy was feeling pretty cocky and proud of himself for the work he'd just done on Carl Appleby. He was clearly in no mood to tolerate pompous, self-important fools. "Mister," he said, "if you *really* want to see my damned badge I'll drop my pants and bend over."

The businessman was appalled. "Why . . ." he stammered, "that's . . . that's filthy and outrageous!"

Billy winked at Longarm. They both struggled up into the wagon and started down the street. The businessman began yelling at them but Longarm and Billy were laughing too hard to hear his words.

Chapter 8

"Water!" the man cried from the backseat of their rented surrey later that morning. "I need water!"

Billy was driving, and they were still a long way from Denver. Longarm twisted around in his seat and pointed his gun at the man's head. "Do you want to shut up . . . or eat a bullet?"

"You can't just murder me!"

"Don't bet on it," Longarm warned.

"Actually," Billy said, "I'm feeling weak and thirsty. Let's pull in at that cafe just a few miles up the road. I've got to get some coffee and breakfast in my belly. I'm so tired and hungry I'm starting to shake."

"Do you have any money left?" Longarm asked.

"No."

"Then what are we supposed to use to pay for our food and coffee?"

Billy frowned. "Search Carl. He's probably got at least a few dollars."

"Then stop for a minute," Longarm said.

Longarm climbed down from the surrey, then reached into their captive's pockets. He found a pocket knife that Billy had somehow missed and decided not to ruin his boss's day by pointing out this important oversight. He also found three dollars and change.

"Hey!" Carl swore. "That's my money! You can't rob me. You're the law!"

"We consider it a loan," Billy told their prisoner. "Besides, you said you were thirsty and we'll use part of your money to buy you a cup of coffee."

"I'd rather have a bottle of whiskey, damn you."

"Coffee is what you'll get if you get anything at all," Longarm said, climbing slowly back into the front seat.

Without glancing over his shoulder, Billy asked, "So what's your name?"

"John Smith."

"No, it isn't. It's Carl Appleby and you were a member of the gang that executed eight innocent people including some women and children."

"No, I wasn't."

Longarm reached into his coat pocket and removed the man's big Bowie knife that he'd taken earlier. "And you used this knife to mutilate Brice, who owned the Bulldog Saloon."

"You're crazy as a loon!"

Longarm slipped the knife out of its beaded sheath and tested the blade on the back of his hand, shaving it clean. "You're going to swing by the neck until you're dead," Longarm said.

"You got no evidence against me!"

"Oh yes, we do. Not only did Brice tell me that you were a murderer, but so did Joe Gorney. Remember him? The fella that you and Jude cheated out of his share of the robbery money?"

"Gorney was lying!"

"No he wasn't, and you'll swing for sure unless . . . ah, never mind."

There was a long silence finally broken when Appleby snarled, "Unless what?"

80

"You might get life in prison if you helped us catch Jude and the rest of the gang."

"I wouldn't squeal on anybody."

"Smart," Longarm said, not bothering to hide his sarcasm. "Real smart. I'm sure that Jude, Hugh Bain, Mad Dog and Mando Lopez will raise a toast when the hangman drops a noose around your neck and you go screaming into hell."

Their prisoner considered this in sullen silence, and then finally asked, "Joe Gorney told you all of our names, huh?"

"That's right," Longarm replied. "And it's only a matter of time before we track every last one of you down."

"You'll have to talk to Satan before he'll let you talk to Hugh Bain."

"He's dead?"

"Jude shot him in the guts for trying to steal more than his share of the bank money."

"Who has the money now?"

"We each got a share. Jude got two shares, him being the leader."

Longarm turned around and stared at their prisoner. "What is Jude's last name and where can we find him?"

"I don't know where any of 'em are anymore. After the bank job we split the take and went our separate ways."

"You're lying," Longarm replied, voice flat and hard. "I know that you and Mad Dog Trabert often saw each other up in Central City. You probably did other bank jobs together that I don't even know about yet."

"No, we didn't! We ... we might have done some stealing up on the mining claims. Maybe even hurt a fella or two, but we never killed anyone again."

"Listen," Longarm said contemptuously. "When I tell the hangman that you were one of the animals that mur-

81

dered all those innocent people, do you know what he'll do?"

"No."

"The hangman has a special way of dealing with particularly bad characters like you," Longarm explained. "He has a way of making the hangman's noose so that it gradually tightens around the neck and slowly strangles you to death."

"No!"

"You ever seen anything strangle?" Longarm asked. "I'm absolutely certain that you're cruel enough to have strangled things before. Do you remember how their faces turned all purple and their limbs were flying this way and that? The sound they made as they choked to death and the way their eyes bugged? How maybe their bowels emptied and—"

"Shut up!"

"That's what this hangman is going to do to you, Carl. He's going to make sure that you die just as slow and hard as any living thing can die. Yes, sir, you can bet that your eyes will bug and—"

"All right!" the man screamed. "I'll cooperate."

"Where can I find Mad Dog Trabert?" Longarm demanded.

"He's in Central City during the summer and he takes off for some cabin up in the higher country during winter when he runs a trap line."

"Where in Central City?"

"There's a woman named Clara Nelson. She rents Trabert a place out back that used to be a workshop and toolshed. She owns a little millinery shop in town."

"What street does she live on?"

"It don't have a name but everyone in town knows Clara. You won't have any trouble finding it."

"Does Trabert have a job?"

"Sometimes. He works whenever he needs some rent

or food money. He finds ways to get his hands on some extra cash."

"He probably rolls drunks and robs houses."

Carl shrugged. "I don't ask. But Trabert gets by. The thing is, though, you can't tell him that I gave you his name. If you did that, he'd find a way to kill me."

"Not if he's behind bars."

"Mad Dog has some tough friends. He'd get one of them to kill me if he couldn't do it himself."

"Don't worry," Longarm assured the man. "We won't tell Mad Dog." He nudged Billy. "I'm feeling hungry myself. Guess when we reach that little cafe, we'll have a couple of big steaks for breakfast. Maybe some flapjacks, eggs and biscuits with gravy."

"I'm real hungry too," Carl whined.

"Too bad," Longarm told his prisoner. "We just don't have enough money for three good breakfast. But we'll feed you when you're locked up in the Denver jail."

Carl cursed them until Longarm reached over the backseat and threatened to smack him across the head with the barrel of his gun. After that, he was quiet and respectful.

When they reached the cafe, Longarm went inside and ordered breakfast while Billy checked Carl's bonds to make sure that he was securely tied up in the backseat. Then Billy joined Longarm for a well-deserved breakfast. There were just three Wyoming cowboys in the cafe and they were laughing and arguing about the weather and who had the smartest cow horse.

"Appleby is going to tell us everything he knows," Billy predicted. "That story you told him about the hangman messing up his noose so he'd strangle was really effective."

"It's no story," Longarm replied. "The hangman's name is Ivan Rostovich. He's a foreigner and rarely talks to anyone."

"Small wonder."

"Ivan hates murderers and when he finds out that this one killed women and children, he would prefer to see Appleby strangle rather than die suddenly of a broken neck."

Billy stared. "Maybe so, but—"

"Ivan would do it," Longarm interrupted. "And who would be there to see the horror of a botched hanging? The governor? Your boss? Not likely. The only spectators would be a few of us who had a hand in bringing Appleby to justice, and do you think we'd raise a stink if Appleby's hanging went sour? Not very damned likely, given the horrible crime he helped commit."

"Let's talk about something else," Billy said as their breakfast plates arrived. "Or I'm going to lose my appetite."

They had a fine breakfast, and when they'd finished their third cup of coffee and couldn't eat another flapjack, Longarm stood up, stretched and said, "We'd better be hitting the road. We've still got a long way to go before we get to Denver."

"I know that," Billy said.

When they stepped out of the cafe, however, both Billy and Longarm had the shock of their lives.

"The surrey is gone!"

They both rushed out into the yard just in time to see Appleby whipping the team of horses over a rolling hill heading north up a dirt road. Longarm shook his head. "What . . ."

"I don't know!" Billy exclaimed, looking devastated. "I thought I had him tied up good and tight."

"He must have had another knife hidden someplace and he cut the ropes," Longarm said. "And if he checked my bag, he'll have found a second pistol I carry for insurance."

Billy shook his head. "I . . . I can't understand it!"

"It doesn't matter," Longarm said. "I'm going to take

that cow horse. It'll be the second one I've confiscated in the past two days. When its owner comes out, tell him I'll be back soon."

"Hold up there, Custis. It's my fault that Appleby got away. Let me go after him!"

"No. You could bust open that side wound and then I'd have two problems instead of just one."

This time, Longarm sized up the horses and chose a tall, clean-legged sorrel gelding that looked as if it could outrun the Wyoming wind. The stirrups looked to be about the right length too. He untied, then mounted the animal and headed off after Carl Appleby. There was little doubt that Billy Vail had lost his edge. But then, that's what vegetating in an office chair would do to even the best of men.

Longarm knew two things. First, the rented team pulling the surrey was exhausted and would not be able to run far, and second, that the horses weren't made for speed even if they had been fresh. So there wasn't much doubt that he would be able to overtake Carl within a mile, two at the most. The only thing that really concerned Longarm is that the man was racing up a dirt road toward a farmhouse. And if he got there before Longarm could stop him, there was no telling what might happen.

"Ya!" Longarm shouted, forcing the sorrel to run its hardest.

The rented surrey left a rooster tail of dust rising up in its wake and Longarm was soon eating dust. Appleby looked around and, sure enough, he had found Longarm's extra Colt because he fired twice.

Longarm couldn't do a thing but watch as the surrey entered the ranch yard. Two people appeared and Longarm watched helplessly as Appleby leaped from the surrey and shoved them into the house just as Longarm swept over a little creek and reined to a hard stop among a stand of big cottonwoods.

Longarm tied his panting horse to the trees and moved over a ways so the animal would not get hit if Appleby insisted on a shootout. Dammit, but this sure wasn't the way that he'd expected things to go!

The hard riding had caused Longarm's head to throb mightily so he leaned his forehead up against a tree and tried to ease the pounding just behind his eyes.

"Marshal!" Appleby shouted from inside the house. "I got a woman and her daughter in here and I'll kill them both if you don't surrender. You know that I will!"

Longarm's head snapped up as a bullet bit into the bark of the cottonwood sending splinters flying. He took a deep breath and shouted, "Give it up, Carl! The others are coming. If you hurt those people, I'll make sure you strangle!"

"I'm going to shoot them right now if you don't come out with your hands up. Do that and I'll let you all live."

"I don't believe you!"

"You got no choice. I'm going to shoot the woman first. I'm going to do it on the count of three."

Longarm heard the woman scream and he closed his eyes desperately trying to decide what to do. If he surrendered, Longarm was sure that Carl Appleby would kill all of them. But, if he didn't give up and the woman and her child were executed while he stood safely behind this tree, then he knew that he'd never forgive himself. That he'd be haunted by their deaths for the rest of his days.

"One!" Appleby shouted. "I ain't bluffing, Marshal. I got nothing to lose by killing 'em both! Two!"

Longarm had no choice but to surrender and take his chances. Otherwise, two innocent victims were going to die.

"All right."

"Come out with your hands high over your head and the gun in your *left* hand!"

Longarm switched the Colt to his left hand. He had shot left-handed before but he wasn't nearly as accurate. "Here

86

I come," he shouted, stepping out from behind the cottonwood. "Don't kill them. No need for them to die."

Appleby pushed a woman out of the house ahead of him, and now Longarm saw that he had a choke hold on a girl of about seven. The girl's hair was the color of corn silk and her blue eyes were enormous pools of terror. Appleby held her around the neck in the crook of his arm and had yanked her up on her tiptoes. The girl looked ready to faint.

"Come on!" Appleby shouted. "Throw away that gun and keep walking."

Longarm did as he was ordered. He could see that the mother was almost hysterical and decided that she would be no help. "Carl, don't hurt them and you still have a chance at life in prison rather than a hangman's noose."

Appleby's eyes were now bright with excitement. "I don't guess that I'll accept either of those choices! That's far enough."

The killer laughed. "You sure picked a bad partner, Marshal. That fool Billy Vail never even bothered to search the inside of my boots. Too bad for you and these two, huh?"

Longarm knew that they were all about to die. But at least now he was in the range of his hidden derringer . . . it had two shots and he'd need them both.

"There's no need to kill the woman and her child," he said, hoping he sounded far calmer than he felt. "Let them go. They mean you no harm."

Appleby sneered and cocked back the hammer of his gun. "I'll have a taste of them both after you've drawn your last breath, you big bast—"

Suddenly, the little girl bit Appleby on the wrist and broke free. Appleby cursed and Longarm fell sideways, rolling twice. His hand sought the derringer affixed to his watch chain. Appleby saw his move and fired. Longarm heard the man's gunshot and felt grit pepper his face as he brought his own stubby weapon up and fired.

They'd both missed but Longarm's second shot struck Appleby in the chest, knocking him backward. The woman screamed again and ran after her child. Appleby staggered and tried to raise his gun and fire at Longarm. He couldn't quite raise it and when he did fire, the bullet ricocheted off the hard gravel. Longarm jumped up and knocked him down with a vicious blow to the face.

Carl Appleby crashed to the earth, a bitter oath on his lips. He died still trying to pull the trigger of Longarm's gun.

The woman rushed over to Longarm and knelt by his side. "Mister," she asked, tears streaming down her face. "Are you *really* a marshal?"

"I am."

"Are you hit?"

"I don't think so."

"But there's blood running down your face!"

"Old wound," he assured her. "Help me up and to a chair, please."

"Is he dead?"

"Yes."

"He was going to kill all of us, wasn't he?"

"I'm afraid so."

"What kind of a man was he, anyhow?"

"A real bad one," Longarm answered, reaching up with his hand.

She helped him over to the house and he waited, head hanging down and blood dripping off his chin into the dirt forming dark little drops.

"Here," she said, dragging out a chair. "Sit down and I'll get you some cool water to drink and . . ."

"I'd rather have whiskey."

A hint of disapproval crossed her face but she said, "I got some."

She disappeared again and her daughter came up to

stare at Longarm sitting in the chair with his head cradled in his hands. In a small voice, she scolded, "You *killed* that man."

"I had no choice."

"The Holy Bible says thou shalt *not* kill."

"I know, but I had no choice," he repeated.

There was a long pause, then the little girl touched his knee and said, "Mama and I are gonna have to do a lot of praying for your soul, Mister."

"I expect that you will. I appreciate it."

"I better go help my mama. I can hear her crying in the house. Papa ain't going to be home 'til suppertime. He can bury the dead man. You too, if you don't live."

"I'd appreciate that as well." He looked up at the small, solemn girl. "Why don't you help your mother find that whiskey."

"She hides it from Pa. She says it's devil's brew."

"Go help her find it anyway."

The little girl dipped her pointy little chin and said, "I expect we're *really* gonna have to pray a lot to get your soul into heaven!"

"I expect you will," Longarm said, seeing two horsemen racing fast up the road. He'd be willing to bet that one of them was Billy Vail and the other was a Wyoming cowboy.

Chapter 9

They'd left Carl Appleby to be buried by the home-
steader's husband, and they'd pushed on back to Denver
not saying much of anything. Longarm was bone tired and
he knew that Billy felt the same way, only even worse
because he'd been responsible for Carl Appleby's near
escape and murder rampage.

"Billy," Longarm said, deep into the night when they
pulled into the Denver livery where they'd rented the
horses and surrey, "quit beating yourself up about what
happened."

"I almost got you and those poor people killed!"

"But you didn't. And when Appleby jumped out of that
Cheyenne hotel window, you were down there to arrest
him."

"He landed so hard he was hurt. I didn't do much of
anything."

"You were a big help," Longarm said. "I couldn't have
done the job alone."

"Bullshit!" Billy said, sounding dejected. "I was a millstone around your neck. I'm not fit to be called a marshal."

Longarm clamped his hand on the man's shoulder.

"There are all kinds of lawmen," he said. "And what you do is important."

"No it isn't," Billy countered. "I'm cheating the American taxpayers who foot my salary."

Longarm was too tired to argue any more. "I'll see you tomorrow at the office. We'll talk about what to do next."

"Sure," Billy said. "See you tomorrow."

Longarm let him go. Billy was feeling awful and there was nothing that could be done this night to change that fact. But tomorrow was a new day and maybe his friend would see things in a better light. After all, he'd tried hard and driven the surrey most all the way up and back from Cheyenne.

When he reached his apartment and unlocked the door, Polly was standing inside with a gun clenched in her shaking hands. Longarm froze, then said, "It's me. Don't shoot. I've had enough trouble already."

Polly dropped the gun and Longarm thanked his stars that it didn't blow a hole in one of them or even the floor. He took the girl in his arms and held her close for a few moments, and then said, "I thought you were staying with the Vail family."

"I did, but then I decided to come over here."

"That's good, but I've got to get some food and some sleep."

"I'll fix you something to eat and draw a bath." She touched his head and felt the matted blood in his hair. "Dr. Carter told me that you shouldn't even be alive, much less going after Appleby. Custis, you look terrible but I'm so glad you're back and alive."

"Half alive . . . maybe," he corrected. "Start the bath water and then the food. I'm going to lie down until they're ready."

He went over to his bed and stretched out. Next thing Longarm knew, the sun was streaming through his windows. Polly had gone off to work but there was warm water just heated for his bath and a clean set of clothes set out for him along with a note that read, *Dear Custis, I love you and will see you either at the office or tonight here at your apartment. Love, Polly.*

Longarm took his bath, shaved and sat down at his table to eat. He felt better but certainly not on top of the world. He wished that he could take a day or two off to recuperate, but now that he knew where Mad Dog Trabert could be found there was no time for delay.

He dressed and checked his weapon, then found a good replacement hat and headed for the office to see Billy Vail. He just hoped that the man was feeling a little more chipper this morning.

The first words out of Billy's mouth after Longarm closed the man's door were, "I can't live with the mistakes I made yesterday. I've decided to turn in my badge and find some other line of employment. Maybe learn to be a gunsmith."

"Billy, have you talked this over with your wife?"

"No. She wouldn't understand."

"Probably not. And to tell you the truth, I think you'd make a lousy gunsmith."

Billy scowled. "I never knew you to kick a friend when he was down."

"You're still a fine marshal," Longarm said. "And I don't want or need a new boss. Some idiot like George Avery would get promoted into your job and then I'd have to quit."

"Now that would be a shame."

"Well, it would happen," Longarm said. Then he said something else that just popped into his mind. "I want you to come up to Central City and help me catch Mad Dog."

Billy couldn't hide his surprise. "After all the mistakes I made with Carl Appleby?"

"Yes."

"Custis, you don't need a millstone tied around your neck again."

"Quit referring to yourself as a damned millstone!" Longarm snapped with genuine irritation. "You made a mistake or two. So what?"

"So what! So what almost got you and that woman and her lovely daughter killed."

"We all make mistakes. I'm sure that you've learned from these most recent ones and that they won't happen again. And I'm not in good shape right now so I could use some backup."

"I'll assign you a deputy marshal."

"No," Longarm said, his voice hard and uncompromising. "The only help I'll accept is yours. Now, will you come with me after Mad Dog . . . or not?"

Billy swallowed and made a pretense of shuffling some papers on his desk. Longarm let the man take his time. He didn't want Billy to do something that the man really didn't want to do or was incapable of doing. On the other hand, he did need help. "Come on, Billy. Quit acting like all that matters is your pride. I need your help arresting Mad Dog. What do you say?"

"All right," Billy finally answered. "And this time I will be a help."

"Good," Longarm said, managing a tired smile. "So what are you going to tell Mr. Ludlow?"

"I don't know but I'll think of something. When can we leave?"

Longarm considered the question. "Mad Dog doesn't know that we know where he lives. So let's give ourselves a day to recover from Cheyenne and Carl Appleby. We can leave tomorrow."

"Suits me just fine. Take the rest of the day off."

"I believe that I will. How about letting Polly take the day off as well?"

Billy shook his head. "You've got a lot of nerve asking

94

me to give her the time off so that you two can spend the day in bed."

"Who said that's what we'd do?"

"I say so."

"You're probably right," Longarm sheepishly admitted. "But most of the time, I'll be sleeping."

"Yeah, sure," Billy said, obviously not believing a word of it.

Early the next morning when Longarm arrived back at the office, the first thing he did was to have a cup of strong coffee. He was still half asleep when Marshal Avery appeared.

"Well ain't you the privileged one," Avery said, coming over to stand beside Longarm. "Me and the others are always here working but you seem to be Mr. Vail's golden boy who can do no wrong. The word is out that not only did you have yesterday off, but so did Miss Raymond!"

"George, I'm just not in the mood to listen to you this morning, so leave me alone."

But Avery was upset and burning with jealousy. "There's also a rumor going around that you are working on that old bank robbery case. That you and Mr. Vail had some kind of privileged information that you're keeping to yourselves. It don't sit right with the rest of us."

Longarm started to turn and walk away but George grabbed his arm. "I ain't done talkin' to you, Custis. We want answers!"

"Here's your answer," Longarm said, pouring his hot coffee across the man's forearm.

George grabbed his arm and howled in pain. "Damn you, Custis!"

Longarm went into Billy's office. Ten minutes later, his boss appeared looking disheveled and upset. "Custis," he demanded, "what's this about you scalding George with coffee this morning?"

"He wouldn't let go of my arm and I taught him a lesson."

"He's got a bad burn. It's blistered!"

"Poor George."

Billy sat down in his desk chair and shook his head. "I don't know how long I can keep you from getting fired. You're messing with Miss Raymond and now you've burned George."

"You can fire me anytime you want," Longarm said, in no mood to apologize. "But first, we ought to go up to Central City and capture Mad Dog Trabert."

"Yeah. I managed to get some emergency travel money. We're fortunate that Mr. Ludlow had to make a quick trip to Washington. Otherwise, we'd have a lot of explaining to do."

"Let's just wrap this case up before he returns and then there won't be nearly so much to talk about. I thought that you'd be wearing some suitable traveling clothes and maybe even packing your sidearm this morning."

Billy climbed out of his chair and went over to a cabinet. He pulled out a valise and said, "My old trail outfit is in here and so is my gun, boots, and badge. I didn't want to raise any eyebrows by looking different. I'll change clothes when we reach Central City."

"Fine," Longarm said. "Are we going to take the morning stagecoach?"

"It would be better if we rented the surrey and horses again," Billy decided. "That way, we wouldn't have to worry about Mad Dog offending or trying to trick any stagecoach passengers on the way back to Denver. How is your head feeling?"

"It's better. How's your side?"

"Healing," Billy told him. He gulped down his own cup of coffee and collected his valise. "I sure wish you hadn't scalded George. I know he can be a real pain, but he tries."

"He ought to try to keep his big mouth shut," Longarm said, finishing the dregs of his coffee and coming to his feet. "The man has a way of getting under my skin. I don't know why you even bother to keep him on the payroll."

"He's Mr. Ludlow's nephew, or weren't you aware of the fact?"

"No, I wasn't," Longarm said with disgust. "But it sure explains a lot of things. What it seems to come down to in this world is not what you do . . . but who you know."

"Not always."

"Pretty near always," Longarm argued as he followed Billy out the door.

Their journey up to Central City was slow, all uphill but uneventful. After boarding their team of horses, they got rooms at the most respectable hotel in town and were so famished that they had a big supper before privately discussing how they would find and capture Mad Dog Trabert.

"The first thing we have to do," Billy reasoned, "is contact his landlord, Clara Nelson, and explain who Mad Dog really is and then find out from her his daily routine. Once we know where he is and what he's doing every hour of the day, we can lay our trap and try to take him by surprise so we don't have to kill the man."

"That sounds reasonable."

"Once the woman understands the gravity of the situation, I'm sure that she will be extremely relieved to see us arrest her tenant."

"No doubt."

Billy seemed pleased that Longarm was so agreeable. "We'll go visit Miss Nelson first thing tomorrow morning. With luck, we'll have Mad Dog in handcuffs by ten

97

o'clock and be on our way back down the mountain."

"That would be great," Longarm said. "With Carl Appleby, Hugh Bain, and Joe Gorney dead . . . and with Mad Dog in custody . . . that would only leave Mando Lopez and the gang's leader, Jude, unaccounted for."

"That's right. I wonder if Lopez crossed the border into Mexico. If he did, we'll have a devil of a time bringing him to justice."

"Perhaps," Longarm said. "Let's just keep our fingers crossed that Mad Dog can tell us where Lopez and Jude are hiding."

"If we keep him alive," Billy said. "That's really important."

"I couldn't agree more."

"Well," Billy added, stifling a yawn, "we ought to go to bed early. We've had another long, difficult day of travel and tomorrow we have to be in peak form."

"I might just mosey around town for a while. Play a little cards and have a couple beers. Nothing wild." Longarm consulted his own pocket watch. "It's only eight-fifteen and that's a bit early for me to go to bed. I wouldn't be able to sleep anyway."

"Suit yourself," Billy said, "but don't get into any trouble, and I expect you to meet me here for breakfast at seven sharp."

"Count on it."

When Billy left the room, Longarm bought a cigar and wandered outside. He found an empty chair on the sidewalk and figured he'd smoke for a while and watch the goings-on of Central City. The town had already seen its best days, but some of its mines were still producing and so the miners still had money in their pockets to spend on liquor and women.

For the next half-hour, Longarm smoked and watched the people moving up and down the street. Sometimes a miner, more often than not inebriated, would plunk down in the empty chair beside him and make small talk or perhaps even ask for beer or whiskey money.

Longarm would always oblige. He didn't mind helping a thirsty man out and, in exchange, he always extracted a bit of information.

"There's a lady named Clara Nelson who owns a millinery shop in this town," he said to one fella more sober than the other. "Do you know where that might be?"

"Why, sure!" one man said after emitting a loud belch. "Miss Nelson's shop is just up the street. I passed it only a few minutes ago. She's still in there working."

"At this late hour?"

"Yep. I saw her and waved through the window. She's a pretty gal. Heard that she lost her husband about two years ago. She's going to make someone a fine young wife. I'd be interested in her myself but I can't be tied down. I like to keep on the move, if you know what I mean."

"Oh," Longarm said, "I know what you mean all right. I keep moving from one place to the next myself."

"You a miner?"

"Nope."

"You don't look much like a cowboy."

"I'm not." Before the man could ask any more questions, Longarm gave him two bits and then decided he might as well mosey down to the millinery shop and have a talk with Miss Nelson. If he could apprehend Mad Dog tonight while the killer was asleep, that would be even better than Billy's daytime plan.

It was almost ten o'clock when he arrived at the millinery store and, sure enough, the young woman was still inside doing some paperwork. He didn't want to disturb her and knew that she might not even respond to his knock, thinking he was just a drunken miner or cowboy looking to get fresh. So Longarm sat on the edge of the boardwalk and continued smoking his cigar. As luck would have it, Clara Nelson finished her work just about the same time he finished his smoke.

"Evening, ma'am," he said, coming to his feet and removing his hat.

She was a fair-haired gal and plenty easy on the eyes. Tall and graceful, Clara Nelson wore a pretty blue dress that probably matched her eyes but the street lamp didn't allow him to be certain of that fact.

"Good evening," she said, locking the door to her shop and starting to move along the boardwalk.

"Ma'am, can I have a quick word with you?"

"No," she said, now hurrying.

He pitched the stub of his cigar into the street and went after her. She glanced over her shoulder, saw him coming, and began to run.

"Ma'am, I'm a United States deputy marshal from Denver!" he called. "I mean you no harm!"

She slowed her pace but did not stop, still unsure if he was being honest or not.

"I can show you my badge." Longarm dug into his pocket. "Turn around and you'll see it in my hand. Don't be afraid. I just need to ask you a few questions."

Clara stopped and turned, hand in her purse. "If you're lying to me and have evil intentions, I have a gun in my hand and I'm plenty willing and capable of using it to defend myself!"

He held the badge out in front and forced a smile. "I shouldn't have frightened you at this hour of the evening but I really need to ask you a couple of questions. I could do that as I walk you home, Miss Nelson."

"*Mrs.* Nelson," she quickly corrected.

"Sorry," he said, meaning it.

She let him come up to her and he said, "My name is Deputy Marshal Custis Long and what I want to know is how I can best capture Mad Dog Trabert alive."

"Who is that?"

Longarm realized his mistake. "He's that fella that is living behind your house. He's probably using an alias but his real name is Trabert and his nickname is Mad Dog."

"I had a renter named Frank Brown."

"Had?" Longarm asked, feeling his heart sink with disappointment.

"Yes. He rented from me for almost three years and then he got drunk and struck me. He was a famous prizefighter once, you know."

"So I heard."

"He had a terrible temper. He would get into fights down in the saloons. I became afraid of him and asked him to find other accommodations. He moved out just five days ago."

"Do you know where he went?"

"I might." Clara began walking. "Just what crime is Mad Dog Trabert supposed to have committed?"

"I don't suppose you get the news from Denver."

"You suppose wrong. I travel to Denver every month to buy new stock and I subscribe to the city's principal newspaper. I have to in order to keep up on current fashions in my business."

"Then maybe you're aware of a terrible bank robbery that took place about five years ago when a bunch of innocent citizens were murdered in cold blood."

She nodded, her expression becoming sad. "I remember because I just happened to be in Denver that week. It was tragic."

"Yes, it was. And Mad Dog Trabert was one of the gang that committed those murders."

They were standing under lamplight and now Longarm could see that Clara was a little older than he'd first thought, but still very attractive. He also thought he smelled liquor on her breath but dismissed that fact as unimportant.

Clara swallowed hard. "And you think that Frank Brown actually helped murder those poor people?"

"I do because we have reliable information. And keep in mind that Trabert would change his name and probably try to act like a law-abiding citizen. But you can't judge a book by its cover and you can't always judge a man . . . or even a woman . . . by appearances."

"I agree."

Two miners out on the town staggered by and doffed their hats, one saying, "Evening, Miss Nelson."

"*Mrs.* Nelson," she corrected.

"Yes, ma'am. Whatever you say."

Clara frowned and when they had passed beyond earshot, she said, "Marshal, why don't you come on to the house and we can have a brandy and talk without fear of being overheard?"

"I'd think that's a fine idea. Especially if you know something that can help me capture Mad Dog. If we can do that, maybe we can get him to tell us where we can find the surviving members of that gang."

"And how many would that be?"

"There were six altogether. I killed one of the gang north of Denver a few days ago. Another one committed suicide in the federal building only last week, and we've recently learned that another was murdered by the gang's leader soon after the crime for attempting to take more than his share of the bank loot."

"So there are just two left?"

"Three, including Mad Dog."

"Well," she said as they began to walk, "I am certainly glad that I didn't marry Frank Brown."

"You were actually thinking of become Mrs. Trabert?"

"Yes, he may be Mad Dog to you, but he's actually quite handsome and charming. We became acquaintances and then good friends. I gave the matter of matrimony serious thought. And I almost married him. We went away

on several trips together . . . and I know that sounds scan-
dalous, but I believe that a man and woman ought to get
to know each other very well before they tie the knot."

"Me too."

"Ministers would certainly disapprove," Clara said,
"but they're also the first ones to insist that a poor woman
stay mired in a terrible marriage because of vows made
in error. Believe me, I know."

"Your marriage wasn't so good, huh?"

"My late husband was a louse. He messed around with
every woman he could charm or pay for. It didn't matter.
I put up with him for fifteen years. He was a lawyer, you
know. They're often not to be trusted."

"Yes, ma'am.

"Anyway, Mr. Nelson was finally shot by an angry husband and he's buried just up the street in the local cem-
etery. Fortunately, he left me with his office building and
a fat bank account. Even so, I knew that I had to find a
way to make a living or I'd eventually be destitute. So I
opened a millinery shop and I've done quite well."

"I'm glad."

"But Frank Brown had big ideas and cash when I first
met him."

"It was most likely his share of the bank's stolen
money."

"He'd convinced me that he'd sold a cattle ranch east
of Denver. He wanted me to sell my house and office
building so we could pool our money and buy another,
large cattle ranch. But I didn't want to live on a ranch,
and now that you've told me Frank's true character, he'd
probably have absconded with my share of the funds and
I'd have been left in a bad situation."

"That's right."

"Are you married, Marshal?"

"No, ma'am."

103

"I'd rather you just called me Clara. What's your first name again?"

"Custis."

"That's a nice, strong name. I like it."

"Thank you."

"Why aren't you married?"

"I just never stayed in one place long enough. I'm too restless."

"That's because you're still young." Clara stopped in front of a white frame house with a picket fence and front porch. "I'll bet you're not even thirty."

"A bit older."

"Marshal, you're aging well. So many men go to pot by the time they're thirty. That's what attracted me to Frank . . . or whatever his real name is . . . he was all man and kept himself physically fit."

"Is this your house?"

"It is. Come on inside and let's have a brandy or two. I think you're a nice man and it's always a pleasure to meet one who is fit and handsome."

"Thank you."

She opened her gate and they went up on the porch. "I sure am glad that I gave Frank the boot instead of marrying him. I'd have been in a terrible mess if he's as corrupt and devious as you say."

"He's worse than that . . . he's a cold-blooded killer."

Clara unlocked her front door. "Well, he may be that," she said, "but he's all man in the sack."

Longarm's eyes widened with surprise and Clara must have seen it because she laughed.

"Have a seat, Custis. I'll get us some libations and be right back."

"Thank you."

Longarm looked around the parlor. It was nice enough, with a grandfather clock and a shelf of books in addition to a comfortable couch and several little tables. He examined the books and other than Shakespeare and a few literary masterpieces by Charles Dickens, Homer and Aristotle, most of the volumes were related to the law.

"My husband loved to read and he was quite an intellectual," Clara said, handing Longarm a glass of brandy, which proved to be excellent. "Sit down."

Clara sat close beside him and sipped her own brandy. "I never cared much for reading. Do you?"

"Not too much." He shrugged. "I never seem to have the time. And, when I do have time, I like to play cards or entertain my friends."

"Men or women friends?"

"Women," he told her. "I prefer the company of the gentler sex."

"And I'll bet they like you as well."

Longarm was too modest to reply. Clara studied his face closely, then said, "Why don't we just stop the chit-chat and go to bed?"

"Excuse me?"

"It's what we both want," Clara said matter-of-factly. "Or at least we would want to after another glass of two of brandy. But liquor can dull the sensations so I'm simply suggesting we just go to bed and enjoy ourselves without the waste of time during meaningless preliminaries."

Longarm wasn't quite sure how to react. After all, it was the man that was supposed to make the advances or seduction, not the woman. And yet, here was this widow being perfectly honest. She wanted to go to bed and make love.

"All right," he agreed, tossing down his brandy. "Why not?"

"Yes! Why not! We can talk about Frank later."

"Fair enough."

She took his hand and led him into her bedroom. The bed was a big, four-poster affair, solid and extra large. Clara wasted no time but turned her bedside lamp low

105

and started to immediately undress. Longarm did the same and when they were both naked as plucked chickens, Clara came into his arms and kissed him hungrily. Her hand snaked down and grabbed his manhood, which was still flaccid.

"Oh, come on, Marshal," she cooed, "you can do far better than that!"

"I sure hope so," he said, cupping her buttocks and lifting her onto the bed.

They began kissing and fondling, and pretty soon Longarm was getting aroused and so was Clara. And when she slid down to take his tool in her mouth, he really started to get in the spirit of the moment.

Clara was very good at what she could do for a man. As Longarm lay on his back with his hands resting on her shoulders, the thought crossed his mind that she had probably had many lovers in her lifetime and the last one had been Mad Dog Trabert. He had to push that thought out of his mind in order to enjoy himself completely and this he accomplished with ease.

When his loins began to ache with a need for release, Longarm had to forcibly pull her up from his crotch.

"Now," she panted, "it's your turn!"

There wasn't much doubt as to what Clara had in mind. Longarm obliged, but when the hungry woman reached down and grabbed his ears and began to push his face so tightly into her wet excitement that he had trouble breathing, Longarm figured he'd had plenty enough of that. Breaking free, he mounted Clara and rode her until she squealed and nearly lost her mind in a fit of ecstasy. Feeling that he'd done his fair share, Longarm slammed his seed up into her until he ran out of juice and then he fell back wet and satisfied.

"Oh my, Custis! You are even better than Mad Dog!"

"Glad to hear it," he gasped. "And while we're on the subject, where can I find him?"

She tweaked his dripping mustache and giggled. "Not so fast, you big, handsome thing you! Come morning, if you treat me right all night, I'll tell you everything you want to know about Frank."

"That's the deal?"

"Yes!" Clara pushed his face down to one of her breasts. "Why don't you make it feel better, honey."

Longarm was beginning to get the picture and he wasn't sure that it was quite as attractive a deal as he'd first thought. Clara Nelson was going to make him earn his information and, unless he was badly mistaken, she was going to get her full measure before the night was finally over.

The next morning, Longarm was so tired that he could barely perform one last time. He really had to work for it and that only made Clara all the happier. When they both finally reached the pinnacle and exploded with cries of pleasure, Longarm collapsed feeling as if he had been sucked almost dry.

"All right," he said, not willing to let the woman out from under him. "You're not moving until you tell me everything you can about Mad Dog."

"Oh, I love to be impaled by a strong man like this! How long can you do it before you go soft and tiny?"

"Never mind that," he told her. "Where is Frank right now?"

"He's up at a little mining settlement about five miles north of us. It's called Rivergold."

"I think I've heard of that strike."

"Frank bought a claim there. He's placer mining."

"Describe him."

"He's tall. Well endowed like yourself."

"I'm not interested in that part of his anatomy. What color is his hair?"

"Brown like yours. He has brown eyes, a beard, and a big smile. Frank has good teeth. Rather long teeth, actually. The first time that I saw him smile I was reminded of a leering wolf."

"And that didn't warn you?"

"No, it excited me. Frank is quite a man. He won't surrender."

"What makes you think that?"

"I know him well. He used to tell me that if he were ever accused and convicted of a crime, he'd never go to prison. He said he'd rather die first. I thought it odd that he would say such a thing at the time because I had no idea of his criminal past. But now I fully understand why he said that and I believe he was sincere. So, if you must face him, do so with the complete knowledge that he will fight to the death."

"There are a lot of tall men up here. Anything else?"

"He has large feet and hands and he wears a gun on his left hip. I asked him why since he is right-handed and he said that he prefers the cross draw. You see, you and Frank have much in common. But you're a better lover."

"Thanks."

"Oh. And Frank likes red flannel shirts. Checked ones, actually. I've rarely seen him wear any other kind. And he usually has a red bandana around his neck. His neck is scarred, you see."

"Maybe someone already tried to hang him."

"Maybe," Clara agreed. "Come to think of it, the scar could have been from a rope. He told me that it was something that he'd received in the war. A slicing saber wound. I thought that made the scar quite romantic."

Longarm could feel his manhood shriveling to a mere shadow of its former self. He climbed off Clara and went to dress.

"Can't you stay a little longer?" she pouted.

"I wouldn't be able to do anything more even if I had all day."

"Oh," she told him, "I don't believe that for a minute.

108

You have excellent recuperative powers, Marshal Long. Just excellent. Did you keep count of how many times we squirted last night together?"

" 'Squirted?' "

"You know. Had our little fountains erupt."

"No, I didn't keep count."

"Five times! No, six including this last one. And each was just as good as the last."

"I hope you are satisfied."

"I'm never completely satisfied. I could handle three men but it might be bad for my health."

"Yes, it might."

"If you see Frank, please don't tell him that I was the one that put you onto his being in Rivergold. That way, if he kills you, he won't come here looking to kill me."

"I doubt that he'd do that, Clara. If he came back, I'm sure that you would seduce and work him down to a nubbin like you did to me last night."

"I certainly would try!"

Longarm left the woman and headed off to meet Billy. He felt weak in the knees and as spent as a empty cartridge. Clara Nelson was the kind that could kill a man if he wasn't physically fit.

Chapter 10

"You're seven minutes late," Billy snapped when Longarm walked into the cafe. "And you've been out carousing all night, haven't you!"

"I got to bed before eleven o'clock."

"The hell you did. Or, if you did . . . it damn sure wasn't to sleep."

Longarm yawned. "What makes you think that?"

"If you could see yourself in the mirror, you wouldn't ask that question. Your eyes look like burnt holes in a blanket and you reek of perfume."

"Well," Longarm conceded, "I was conducting business."

"Sure you were."

"With Mrs. Clara Nelson."

Billy had been about to put his coffee cup to his lips but now he set it down with a loud clatter. "You spent the night with Clara Nelson!"

"Shhh!" Longarm breathed. "Billy, will you keep your voice down. Clara has to live and do business in this town. We don't want to besmirch her reputation."

"Yeah," he said, lowering his voice. "You go out and

bed her down in a matter of minutes. What kind of a reputation is she likely to have anyway?"

"You always were a grouchy sonofabitch first thing in the morning," Longarm said. "What did you order for breakfast?"

"Steak. Eggs over easy. Flapjacks. The works for one dollar."

"Sounds good to me. Think I'll have the same." Longarm got up and went over to the counter to order and to get a cup for his coffee. When he returned to the table, Billy was still steaming.

"I don't understand how or why you tomcat around so much," Billy said.

"You're just jealous. And anyway, our man has fled the coop."

"Mad Dog is gone?"

"Yes. He tried to trick Clara into selling her properties and handing him a wad of money to buy a cattle ranch. When she refused, he struck her and she insisted he leave."

"From what we know, she's lucky he didn't beat her to death."

"That crossed my mind too. Anyway, he didn't go far. Clara says that Mad Dog is working a mining claim just up the canyon at a strike called Rivergold."

"I've heard of Rivergold."

"We can go up there this morning and catch him by surprise. Maybe we'll get lucky and he'll be up to his knees in a freezing streambed and won't have any choice but to surrender."

"That would be a refreshing change. You can't keep killing them."

Longarm sampled his coffee. "I've never shot a man that didn't either deserve or force me to shoot him."

"I know. I know." Billy sighed. "It's just that we have to take him alive."

"That's true," Longarm agreed. "But there's something even more important that you need to remember."

"And that is?"

"We have to stay alive ourselves."

Billy smiled. "You're right. Better Mad Dog gets it than either of us."

Their breakfast arrived and Longarm was famished. He devoured his breakfast, then had another cup of coffee before he talked Billy out of one of his cigars.

"Why don't you pay up and I'll meet you at the hotel after I clean up a bit and shave."

"What difference does it make now?" Billy asked. "You've had your nightly conquest. All we're going to do now is try to capture a killer."

"You're probably right." Longarm rubbed his stubble. "But all the same I think I'll go up to my room and shave. I'll meet you down in the lobby in a half-hour."

"Okay," Billy said. "I sure hope this capture will be easy."

"Don't count on it," Longarm replied. "Clara told me that he'd bragged he'd never be taken alive."

"She knew he was a killer?"

"No. But I think she suspected it," Longarm said as he got up and headed off to their hotel.

Clara was standing in front of the hotel waiting when he showed up and the moment she saw him, she smiled. "I thought I'd wish you well up in Rivergold."

"Thanks."

"There's something else I wanted to say."

"What's that?"

"You were wonderful last night and I would love a repeat. Tonight I could cook you . . ."

Longarm placed his hand on her arm. "Clara, my boss and I are going up the canyon to try and arrest Mad Dog. You tell me he's vowed never to be taken alive. So let's just see what happens. If it all goes well, maybe we can

113

get together and have a private celebration."

She leaned forward and kissed him on the lips. "Do you work at the federal building in downtown Denver?"

"Yes. It's on the corner of Cherokee and Colfax. The U.S. Marshal's Office is upstairs."

"Assuming you survive and capture Frank, may I come by the next time I'm shopping in Denver and pay you a visit?"

Longarm thought of Polly and knew that Clara's visit would cause a lot of tongues to start wagging. "I . . . uh, I guess."

"You don't sound very excited about it," she said. "Is it because you have another woman who might object?"

"Yes."

She frowned. "How very disappointing. Is there any other fit marshal like yourself?"

Longarm thought a moment then had an inspiration. "There is a fella named George Avery."

"Perhaps I should ask for him."

"He'd like that, Clara. George is very interested in meeting a lovely and healthy young woman like yourself."

"And he's not married or romantically involved?"

"Not that I know of."

Clara smiled. "Then I'll seek out Mr. Avery. And, if he is unsuitable . . . well, who knows? By then you might be unencumbered by a woman and want to do a repeat performance of last night. Eh?"

"I sure might!"

"Good." Mrs. Clara Nelson stepped back, straightened and said, "I wish you the very best of luck up in River-gold. Please be careful. Frank won't hesitate to kill you."

"I'm aware of that, Clara."

Her eyes filled with tears. "If only Frank had been an honest, decent man! We really had such a great time in the old sack!"

114

And then, she hurried away leaving Longarm to shake his head.

Longarm and Billy hitched up their rented surrey and headed up the canyon. It took only a little more than one hour to reach the new mining claim called Rivergold where men were swarming all over a stream panning for gold. There were three tent saloons and a couple of open supply stores where business was conducted over a plank of wood laid across two empty whiskey barrels.

"We'll leave the surrey here and walk through the camp," Longarm said.

"Do you think we can afford to leave it without a guard?" Billy asked. "This place looks pretty rough."

"It is rough but this shouldn't take long. Clara gave me a good description of Mad Dog and I expect he'll be easy to spot. He likes to wear red flannel shirts, and a red bandana. He wears his gun like I do and is tall. Brown hair and brown beard. I'll spot him easy enough."

"I hope so," Billy said, nervously checking his gun once more.

Billy looked so worried that Longarm decided it might be better if he remained with the horses. "You know something," Longarm said, "maybe it would be smarter if you stayed here to guard our horses and surrey. All I'm going to have to do is spot Mad Dog, then walk up and draw my gun. He'll either surrender or I'll shoot him."

"If you shoot him, make it in the leg. Or better yet the foot."

But Longarm shook his head. "With someone as deadly as Mad Dog, you always shoot to kill."

"All right."

Longarm gave Billy a smile. "Relax. I'll find the man, get the drop on him and we'll be back in less than an hour."

"What if he goes for his gun?"

115

"I expect that, but I'll already have mine out and I'll use it to crack his skull a good one. That will be the end of the matter."

"Good luck."

"Thanks," Longarm said, starting off. "But if you should hear shooting, it might be a good idea to come running."

"Don't worry, I will."

Longarm started down through the collection of rough tents and saloons. He guessed there were maybe a thousand men in Rivergold, perhaps even more. They were either miners or merchants and, as in most mining towns, the merchants looked to be the more prosperous.

"Hey, fella, we got good whiskey over here!" a grinning man wearing a bar apron called. "You won't find better value for your gold dust!"

Longarm kept on moving. Several merchants called out for him to stop and buy their wares but he paid them no mind. There were plenty of tall men in this town and most had brown hair and beards. Red flannel shirts were also commonplace so Longarm kept thinking, *red bandana. Gun on his left hip, butt forward to be used in a cross draw*.

When he had looked at every last face in the settlement, Longarm was left with the mining claims and he knew this part of the search would be trickier. You had to be extremely careful about moving through the claims because the miners were very unfriendly to trespassers. Even so, there were usually safe alleyways between the claims leading down to the stream and they were defined by well-worn footpaths.

Longarm tried to look inconspicuous as he moseyed along, smiling at men who stared at him with cold, suspicious eyes.

"Don't step a foot on my claim," a man with shoulders

like a buffalo warned. "If you do, I'll grab your leg and twist it off!"

Longarm didn't appreciate the threat but he didn't think it wise to argue the matter, either. So he watched his step and moved slowly through the claims, eyes missing no one.

The shallow stream was fifty yards wide. There were prospectors everywhere and how they exactly defined their particular claims was interesting. Some piled rocks up in mounds to delineate their boundaries. Others had pounded sharpened sticks and poles into the gravel stream-bed. But many of the claims were unmarked, no doubt causing frequent fistfights and gun battles.

Longarm stood on the bank of the stream and began to scrutinize every living soul until his eyes came to rest on one of the largest prospectors. He stood out with a red bandana tied around his neck, and a red flannel shirt. Even more distinctive was the gun strapped on his left hip, butt forward. Longarm was sure that this was Mad Dog Trabert alias Frank Brown.

So now the decision was to either go out there and make the arrest or to wait until the killer came ashore, then to sidle up and get the drop on him.

"Oh hell," Longarm whispered. "I might as well get this over with."

He waded into the stream and didn't even bother to try and figure out the unmarked claim boundaries. Men cursed at him and one tried to push him sideways but Longarm shoved the man over backward and plodded on across the stream, which was swift but only about two feet deep. Mad Dog hadn't noticed him yet and when Longarm entered the fugitive's claim, he drew his six-gun and shouted, "I'm United States Marshal Custis Long and you are under arrest for murder!"

Mad Dog was bent over with his gold pan full of sand and water. Without even looking up, he hurled the pan and its contents straight into Longarm's face. If it hadn't been for the fact that he desperately needed to take this man alive, Longarm would have opened fire. Instead, he tried to clear his eyes with his left forearm.

That was a mistake because Mad Dog hit him in the side of the jaw so hard that Longarm landed in the water. The next thing he knew, the ex–bare-knuckle fighter had kicked the gun out of his hand and was astraddle his chest, fists slamming down into Longarm's face. Then Mad Dog grabbed Longarm by the throat and tried to twist his face sideways and push it underwater so that he'd drown.

Longarm was in a bad fix. The man was so big and strong that the only thing Longarm could do was to grab his own fistfuls of gravel and hurl them into Mad Dog's eyes. That slowed but did not stop the crazed killer so Longarm hooked his heels around the man's head, then yanked him over backward.

Dazed and bloodied by the punches he'd taken and still fighting to clear his own vision, Longarm was losing the fight. He still had his vest pocket derringer and he was damn sure going to use it if this fight didn't turn in his favor real quick.

They came to their feet, both trying to clear their vision. Longarm figured that he was outclassed when Mad Dog punched him three times so hard and fast that he was knocked back down again. Mad Dog dove at him with his knees drawn up, intending to knock the wind from his lungs. Longarm grabbed a fist-sized rock and struggled to his feet. As his opponent was trying to stand, Longarm struck Mad Dog just over the right eye with the rock, peeling his brow away like the skin of an apple.

Mad Dog's eyes lost their focus and Longarm slammed him with a tremendous uppercut that brought him to his knees. Now Longarm was in command and, with the dim realization that hundreds of prospectors were screaming and cheering, Longarm pounded Mad Dog's face as hard and as fast as he could swing his fists.

But Mad Dog wasn't finished. He ducked a punch, then jumped up shouting, "Come and get it, Marshal!"

They stood toe to toe in the freezing water trading vicious punches. Longarm's face was already so numb and battered that the punches didn't hurt but he could feel himself giving ground. He blocked a haymaker, lowered his shoulder and slammed it into the bank robber. They fell rolling and clawing, twisting and gouging. Mad Dog had Longarm in a headlock and was trying to break his neck. Longarm found another rock and blindly hammered Mad Dog three times right between the eyes. The killer released his choke hold.

Longarm knew that he had to win quickly or he stood no chance. So he grabbed a second rock and while Mad Dog was still dazed, he threw his arms out wide, then slammed both rocks into each of the outlaw's ears. Mad Dog collapsed face down. Longarm let him stay that way for almost a minute as he swayed with exhaustion. Then, he dropped the rocks, grabbed Mad Dog by the collar and lifted his head out of the water.

"Marshal, did you kill that ornery sonofabitch?" someone asked as Longarm dragged his fugitive across mining claims to the shore. "That was one hell of a fight!"

Longarm dropped Mad Dog in the mud. Struggling to get his wind back, he panted, "There's a man waiting beside a surrey just up the road a short ways. Tell him to come running."

"Yes, sir! You sure look bad, Marshal. Face is swelling like you got bit by a rattlesnake."

Longarm sat down on the bank and fumbled for his derringer. He was more than a little surprised that it hadn't been torn loose during the fight. When he had it in his fist, he rolled Mad Dog onto his back. The man was bleeding from his mouth, ears and nose. His handsome face was now anything but handsome.

"Mad Dog, you'd have saved us both a lot of trouble if you'd just gone ahead and surrendered," Longarm told the unconscious figure as he searched him and removed two knives, a Colt and a derringer just like his own.

"He's a bad one," one of the crowd who had gathered around said. "Everyone in Rivergold hates Frank Brown and gives him a wide berth. He's already killed two prospectors. Thought for sure that you were going to be number three!"

"I almost was," Longarm said, washing the blood from his own face with handfuls of water. "His name isn't Frank Brown, though. It's Mad Dog Trabert."

"What'd he do?"

"He and some of his friends robbed a bank and shot to death not only men . . . but also innocent bystanders which included women and children."

"Why don't you let us string him up right now?"

This suggestion was met with great enthusiasm. Someone yelled for someone else to hurry up and find a rope.

"There will be no lynching," Longarm yelled as loud as his strength permitted. "We're taking him back to Denver where he'll not only stand trial, but we hope he'll tell us where we can find the remaining members of his gang."

The prospectors didn't like that idea even a little bit. Someone came running up the stream with a big rope in his hand and they found a thick branch on one of the nearby cottonwood trees. Fortunately, Billy arrived just about then and took control of the situation because Longarm was just too whipped to do much of anything except clear his head. He didn't have a pair of handcuffs so he rolled Mad Dog over on his back again and Billy tied him hand and foot with his own red suspenders.

"All right you men, help us carry this murderer up to our wagon!" Billy shouted.

"Are you sure he won't be set free when you get him to Denver?" a prospector demanded to know.

"I give you my word he will hang," Billy yelled. "Hell, I'll even send word up here where and when it will happen if you boys want to come and watch!"

This offer was met with far more enthusiasm and the prospectors gladly helped haul the still unconscious murderer up to the surrey.

"Dump him in the backseat," Billy said, helping Longarm up beside him in the front. "You all right?"

"Never felt better," Longarm deadpanned.

"I should have come and helped," Billy said. "It appears to me that he beat the living hell out of you."

"That's close to the truth."

"Just sit still and we'll go on back down to Central City and find you both a doctor."

Longarm twisted around and stared at their unconscious prisoner. "I might have busted his skull. That's what I wanted to do when we were fighting."

"If you did, then Mad Dog will be no use to us."

"I know, but better his skull than mine." Longarm turned back around to the front. "That's about the toughest man I ever fought."

Billy drove the team through the crowd and back out on the road that would take them down to Central City. "Custis, why didn't you just get the drop on him like you planned?"

"Well, I tried to but he was real fast."

"When we get to Central City we'll get some rope and tie him up so tight that he won't even be able to wiggle . . . that is . . . if he don't die on us first. When a man is bleeding from the ears like that, it often means that his skull is broke and he's finished. You aren't bleeding from the ears . . . are you?"

"If I'm not it's about the only place on my head that isn't leaking blood."

"I sure should have come along with you," Billy said. "If I had, there wouldn't have been a fight."

"Yes, there would have," Longarm answered. "There's just too much fight in the man to give up peaceably. I have a feeling it's like Clara said . . . he'd rather die than go to prison or to the gallows."

"He might die," Billy said fretfully, glancing over his own shoulder. "He looks real bad. His face is as white as milk. What did you hit him with besides your fists?"

"Rocks. I hit him between the eyes and I bashed in both ears." Longarm flexed his fingers. "He has a jaw like granite and a head like a cast-iron stove. I couldn't do anything with my hands except break all my knuckles. That's why I used the rocks."

"Well," Billy said, "they sure did the job. Hear him breathing so hard like that?"

"Yeah."

"Means he's dying. I think we'll wind up burying the bastard in Central City. That's what I think will happen. Dammit! I sure should have gone and helped you get the drop on him!"

Longarm glanced back over his shoulder again. Mad Dog Trabert's face was unrecognizable and Billy was right, the man was laboring to breathe. *Man,* Longarm thought, *I sure hope I didn't kill him.*

Chapter 11

Their arrival back in Central City caused quite a stir and people stopped whatever they were doing to stare at the two battered figures riding in the surrey. Billy was feeling so guilty that Longarm didn't have the heart to tell his boss that there wasn't any doctor to examine him or their unconscious prisoner.

"Custis, you're in no condition to go any farther today so we'll get a hotel room tonight and head on down to Denver in the morning," Billy said as he drove up the main street ignoring the shouted questions.

Longarm didn't bother to disagree. He figured a good night's sleep was necessary if he were to make it back to Denver.

"Custis!" Clara Nelson shouted, pushing through the curious crowd to rush up beside the surrey. Her hand flew to her mouth and her eyes widened as she stared at the figure in the backseat. "Custis, what . . . Frank? Is that Frank?"

"His name is Trabert," Billy snapped. "Miss, would you please stand back so you don't get your foot run over by a wheel."

But Clara wasn't listening. "Custis!" she wailed. "What did you and Frank do to each other?"

"We got into a fight."

"Is he . . . dying?"

"I don't know." Longram shook his head. "Clara, is there anyone here in town that would even remotely qualify as a doctor?"

"There's Ian MacTavish. He pulls teeth. Stitches up wounds, delivers an occasional baby and tends to sick and injured horses."

"We're going to need him," Longarm told the woman.

Billy drew their team up in front of the hotel. Without looking at anyone in particular, he shouted, "We need some help to get this man inside!"

Nobody offered to help. Maybe they didn't want to get blood all over themselves, which seemed reasonable to Longarm.

"We're United States marshals and the man in the backseat is a murderer!" Billy thundered. "Now would a couple of you men give us a hand?"

Two strong miners came forward. Under Billy's supervision, they eased Mad Dog out of the surrey and carried him into the hotel.

"You better come with me," Clara said, trying to help Longarm out of the surrey.

"No. I have to stay with Billy just in case Mad Dog survives and tries anything."

" 'Tries anything?' " Clara echoed with astonishment. "Custis, anyone can see that he's dying."

"Maybe, but he's the toughest man I ever tangled with and I wouldn't want him to wake up in the middle of the night to murder Billy."

"But he's tied up!"

Longarm eased out of the seat and stood feeling quite unsteady. "Clara, go find MacTavish and tell him to bring whatever medicine he has. What he can't use on Mad Dog he can use on me."

"You should have shot Frank. That's what you should have done."

"Yeah," Longarm said wearily. "But I needed to take him alive so he can help us find the other bank robbers. Remember?"

"I know, but just look at your face. You look awful!"

"I'll heal." Longarm was in no mood to argue. "Would you please go find MacTavish?"

"He won't be able to do a thing for Frank, but he might be able to help you," Clara said, clearly unhappy about being sent away.

Several men helped Longarm into the hotel. The desk clerk was very upset about bringing Mad Dog inside and didn't want him to mess up a perfectly good set of bedsheets. Billy finally had to threaten the man with arrest before he would hand over a room key. People were shouting and there was a lot of confusion as Longarm and Billy led the procession down a hallway to their room.

"This fella is as good as dead," one of the miners said. "You want us to put him on the bed?"

"No," Billy told him. "Lay him out on the floor. And thanks for your help."

"That's Frank Brown," one of them said, bending over the unconscious man's battered and bloodied face. "Don't look much like him anymore, though. He was a mean bastard. Marshal, there ain't a man in Central City that wouldn't just as soon see him die."

"I know." Longarm eased the miners out of their room, adding, "We need him to help us find out who else robbed a bank in Denver and shot eight people to death."

"You might try lighting a match and burning his bare toes," one of the miners suggested. "That could bring him around for awhile."

125

"Good idea," Longarm said, "but it wouldn't be right to torture a helpless man."

"Frank Brown never knew a helpless day in his life. He could whip any two men in Central City and it's a wonder that he didn't kill you. That makes you a hero, Marshal."

They said more but Longarm eased them out into the hallway and shut the door. Then he collapsed on one of the two narrow beds and closed his eyes.

"What about a doctor?" Billy asked.

"There are no doctors in this town, but Clara said there was a man named Ian MacTavish who could help us. I sent her off to find him."

"No doctor." Billy shook his head and knelt beside Mad Dog and studied their prisoner. "His breathing sounds real bad and I just checked his pulse, which is fast and weak. I don't think he'll pull through."

"He's amazingly strong," Longarm said. "He could surprise us."

"All I want is information on the last two members of that bank holdup gang. If we get that much, he can die any damned time he pleases."

"Generous of you to allow him that privilege," Longarm said, closing his eyes.

He fell asleep but not for long because the next thing Longarm knew, a short, bearded man in his fifties wearing spectacles was standing over him, gently dabbing ointment on his facial cuts and bruises.

"Just rest easy, lad," the man said in a thick Scottish brogue. "You're going to be fine."

"You'd be Ian," Longarm said.

"Aye. Now rest easy. You have taken quite a beating."

Clara came into view. "Ian says that Frank probably won't live until morning."

"How sure are you of that?" Longarm asked.

"Not sure at all," MacTavish admitted. "The human

126

body is an amazing piece of chemistry. And, I'm not a real doctor, though I studied medicine for a while in Scotland. Brain injuries are always a mystery and almost impossible to treat. I do know that he has some cranial bleeding and that means deadly pressure is being applied to the man's brain. My opinion is that he'll not last until morning. But, if he does, then I'd say he has a good chance for survival."

"I just need to talk to him for a few minutes," Billy said. "He's the only one that can help us find the other members of his gang."

MacTavish shrugged his round shoulders, removed and polished his spectacles. "I have some very strong smelling salts. We could try them and see if that revives the man."

"What have we to lose?" Billy asked.

"Nothing."

"Then bring them out and let's see if they work," Billy told the Scot.

MacTavish had a medical kit that was packed with bandages and supplies. After much rummaging around he found the smelling salts and held the small, corked vial up for everyone to see. The liquid inside was thick and yellowish in appearance.

"What is it?" Longarm asked.

"It's the scent gland extracts of a large skunk." MacTavish managed a smile. "Very unpleasant and quite difficult to obtain."

"I should imagine."

"Before I open the vial," MacTavish said, "I would suggest we drag the patient over beside the window and make sure that it is opened wide."

"Good idea," Billy told the man.

They wrestled the unconscious killer over to the window and propped him up against the wall.

"Here we go," MacTavish said, uncorking the vial,

finding a cotton ball and then saturating it with the skunk scent.

Everyone in the room recoiled except MacTavish at the powerful and unpleasant scent.

"That would rouse a corpse!" Billy cried, crabbing toward the door with Clara right on his heels.

Longarm felt his eyes burn, but the horrific odor did clear his head. He watched as Mad Dog's body jerked and then, in utter amazement, saw the killer's eyelids flutter.

"It's working!" MacTavish exclaimed, his own eyes bleeding tears.

Mad Dog's head began to roll back and forth on his shoulders and MacTavish kept the cotton ball right under his nostrils. Finally, the man's eyes blinked open and stared. He coughed and drool ran from the corner of his mashed lips.

Longarm grabbed him by the front of his shirt. "Mad Dog. Where are Jude and Mando Lopez?"

The prisoner wasn't really conscious. At least, he wasn't thinking clearly or he probably would have spit in Longarm's face. Instead, he groggily mumbled something unintelligible.

"I have to stop," MacTavish said, retreating from Longarm and the killer. "I can't take this smell for another minute."

Longarm snatched the cotton ball from MacTavish's hand and practically rammed it up one of Mad Dog's nostrils. "Where are Jude and Mando Lopez?"

The semiconscious killer had the dry heaves. His head rolled back and forth on his wide shoulders and, in a tortured voice, he spewed out a stream of curses and garbled words. Only one word echoed clearly in Longarm's mind. He released Mad Dog and rocked back on his haunches. Turning toward the doorway, he stared at Billy and asked, "Did you hear that?"

"Yes, they're up in Laramie. By jingo, we've got

128

them!" Billy cried. "I'll bet that's where Carl Appleby was heading when we caught and killed him."

"It makes sense, doesn't it," Longarm said, tossing the odious cotton ball out the window. "So now we take Mad Dog down to Denver if he survives the night and then I go up to Laramie."

"We *both* go to Laramie," Billy corrected. "I haven't come this far to let you go it alone now. Besides, you need my help. You need a doctor's help."

MacTavish had overheard the conversation and said, "if he lives through this night, your prisoner would never survive a trip down to Denver."

"Custis," Billy decided after a moment of consideration. "Why don't we get some sleep? We can make some intelligent decisions based on whether Mad Dog is dead or alive tomorrow morning."

"We can't stay in this room," Longarm said. "You'll need to go back down to the desk clerk and rent a second room."

"I suppose that's true," Billy agreed. "Though I hate to waste the money. And who is going to guard Mad Dog tonight if we are sleeping in another room?"

"We'll tie him up good and tight," Longarm suggested.

"You could stay with me again," Clara whispered in Longarm's ear. "Even looking like you do I would still love you back in my bed."

"Another time," Longarm told her. "Could you find us some rope?"

His response hadn't been the one she'd wanted or expected. "What am I?" Clara snapped in exasperation. "Your personal step-and-fetch-it?"

"You're far more important than that. But we badly need rope."

"All right," she said, heaving a deep sigh of resignation. "I'll get some from the merchantile. But I'm not paying for it out of my pocket. I need money."

Billy gave her four bits and Clara disappeared.

"How much do we owe you, Doc?" Billy asked the Scot.

"One dollar. If your prisoner dies, you're going to need to pay the mortician." He stuck out his jaw. "I don't do that kind of work for free, you know."

"You're also the mortician?" Billy asked, looking surprised.

"Sure. That way, when they're badly hurt, I earn a fee either way. No crime in that, is there?"

"I suppose not," Billy said, not looking pleased. "But it does seem like a conflict of interests. I mean, you probably make more as a mortician than as a doctor, don't you?"

"Aye! I make good caskets and expect to be paid well for my trouble."

Billy paid the Scot and he left. Clara soon returned and they removed Mad Dog's suspenders from his hands and feet. Longarm was kneeling beside their prisoner when he turned his head to say, "Clara, you can hand me that rope now."

Suddenly, Mad Dog lashed out with his boot and hit Longarm in the temple. Clara shrieked and Longarm heard the sound of flesh striking flesh. He tried to recover, but Mad Dog was already tearing his sidearm from its holster.

"Freeze!" Billy cried.

Two guns exploded together in that skunk-stinking hotel room. Billy heaved a deep sigh and said, "Well, at least now we won't have to worry about tying up Mad Dog and taking him down to Denver to stand trial."

That's when Longarm saw the blood-leaking bullet hole punched between Mad Dog's glazing eyes.

Chapter 12

Longarm wasn't fit to travel the next morning. His face was discolored, his ribs ached and both of his eyes were nearly swollen shut.

"You go ahead on down to Denver," he suggested to Billy. "I'll recuperate for a few more days and hitch a ride with one of the supply wagons. Maybe I can even talk Clara into taking me down on an early buying trip."

Billy had been pacing back and forth in their hotel room. "I paid MacTavish to bury Mad Dog. The man wanted to give him a nice casket but I told him that Mad Dog didn't deserve anything but a pauper's burial in a plain wooden box. MacTavish wasn't pleased but he did the job for ten dollars. No headstone and no wooden cross. Just a rock with his name painted on it in white letters."

"That's more than Mad Dog deserved," Longarm said. "Why don't you drive the surrey down to Denver and report in at the office before we're both fired for our absence."

"When I do I'll have to tell Mr. Ludlow the truth and I doubt he'll be happy."

"Why wouldn't he be?" Longarm asked with surprise.

"We've managed to kill two members of the gang and we're hot on the trail of the last pair."

"Mr. Ludlow will be upset when he realizes that we went ahead and acted without his approval. He insists on approving everything. That's especially true of something as important as solving that bank robbery and murder case."

"Billy," Longarm said, "you can handle the man. Tell him that we'll definitely take the leader named Jude as well as Mando Lopcz alive. And when we return them to Denver for trial, Ludlow can get all the favorable publicity and we won't take credit for anything."

"Yeah," Billy said, still looking worried. "That's about how I figured I'd handle him. If we can make Ludlow look good in the newspapers, then we don't have a problem. But he's going to want us to get right up to Laramie and close this out."

"I know," Longarm said. "But I need at least a few days to recover. My head is still ringing and I feel like I've been run over by a stampede of Longhorn cattle."

"That must have been one hell of a fight you had with Mad Dog. I blame myself for not being there to help."

"You more than redeemed yourself yesterday when you killed Mad Dog. He had my gun and he would have shot us all if you hadn't gotten him first. That showed me you still have what it takes to be out in the field. Billy, you really saved our lives."

Billy couldn't help but swell a bit with pride. "I . . . I guess I did act pretty quickly and decisively."

"You were amazing," Longarm said. "So drive the surrey on back down to Denver and I'll come along in three or four days at the most. I've earned that much, haven't I?"

"You're the best," Billy said. "And I can't tell you how much it's meant to me to be working with you again after all those years riding a desk chair. Now that I've had a taste of what it means to be out in field again chasing criminals, I'm not sure that I can go back to the office and play politics."

"I understand."

Billy gathered his bags and started to leave. "Oh, by the way, Miss Clara Nelson is waiting down in the lobby. I told her that we needed a few words in private and then she could come up and take care of you. I think she wants to move you over to her house."

"I'd like that."

Billy shook his head. "I thought you might. But try to get some rest, Custis. You're in no shape to be humping that woman both day and night when you're supposed to be convalescing."

"I couldn't agree more." Longarm tried to wink but it didn't work.

Billy chuckled. "You're a marvel, Custis. A living monument to sexual overindulgence."

"Perhaps, but you have to admit that it wouldn't be a bad way to check out."

"No," Billy grudgingly agreed, "it sure wouldn't."

A short time later as Clara was helping Longarm up the street, Billy drove past in the surrey and yelled, "You're a crazy fool and it's gonna kill you one of these days!"

"Then at least I'll die with a big smile on my face!" Longarm shouted back at the man.

Billy said something else but by then he was heading along at a good clip so Longarm didn't hear the words. It was probably just as well.

Clara bathed and fed him and then she tucked him into bed and whispered, "I've got to go open my shop. But I'll be back at noon for lunch and guess what we'll have?"

"What?"

"Each other," Clara said, breaking into giggles.

Longarm smiled through his purple lips and watched

Clara go off to work. He dozed and when Clara returned, she came right to bed and, by being careful, Longarm was able to perform to his own credit. He performed so well that Clara wanted seconds but he convinced her that she'd get another go at him in the evening.

"I'm going to cook steaks and we'll drink good red wine. Red wine is a blood enhancer and it gives a man lots of stamina," Clara told him. "Red wine at night and lots of cold milk in the morning. Between the two of them, a fit man can perform far beyond what is normal."

"No kidding," Longarm said, with more than a little interest. "Any proof of that?"

"Sure. Frank was the one that told me that secret and he was living proof that they worked wonders on a man's body."

"Well then, bring on the wine and the morning milk," Longarm told her.

She reached under the sheets and wiggled his worm. "Don't worry, honey. We're going to have some good times in the week ahead!"

"Clara, I can't stay a whole week."

Her grip on his privates tightened. "Sure you can, darling. And then I'll drive you down to Denver and you'll be looking and feeling like a new man."

Longarm was in no position to argue so he nodded and kissed Clara good-bye.

The next week passed so swiftly that it would have been perfect if he hadn't fretted about not keeping his promise to Billy to arrive in Denver after a few days. Still and all, his body was in need of rest and Clara's conviction that lots of red wine at night and and cold milk in the morning could enhance a man's sexual prowess did need to be proved . . . or disproved. As it turned out, Mad Dog had been correct.

"I have to get back to work," Longarm finally said.

"Clara, as much as I'd like to, I just can't put it off any longer. I've been here a full week."

"I know." They were lying in bed gazing out her bedroom window at the break of day. "But I'm not ready to go on a buying trip yet, and I've spent so much work time with you that my business has really suffered."

"I'll catch a ride with someone," he told her. "Don't worry."

"Are you sure?"

"I am. I feel great. You know that I do."

She nuzzled his neck. "I'll come down and visit you in about three weeks. All right?"

"Of course."

"And you won't let yourself get killed or all beat up again when you go after Jude and Mando Lopez?"

"I'll sure try not to," he told her.

Clara kissed his lips tenderly. "Then let's make love one last time and I'll let you go."

Longarm thought that was a damn fine idea.

He'd caught a ride down to Denver with a talkative young muleskinner named Dave Yocum, whose groaning freight wagon was heavily laden with lumber from Central City's only sawmill.

"When I was a kid I used to think I was either going to be an outlaw or a marshal like yourself," Yocum announced not long after the start of their journey down the mountain. "That I'd live either on one side of the law or the other."

"But instead you became a freighter."

"I did." Young Yocum spit a long stream of tobacco juice straight ahead and it sliced neatly between the two nearest animals. "I like mules and I like being outdoors. Best of all, I like getting paid."

"We don't make a lot of money," Longarm told the congenial young man, "but it's not terrible. And, I'm almost always on assignment chasing some outlaw."

"I'd like that," Yocum said. "I'm a real good rider and a crack shot with either a rifle or a pistol."

"That's important. We also need marshals who can react without panic in a tight fix."

"I'm pretty coolheaded," Yocum announced. "Once, my wagon's brake wouldn't work on the worst of downgrades. I could see that the mules were going to get run over and then me and the whole works would go flying into a deep gorge."

"So what did you do?"

Yocum shook his head. "I am sad to tell you but I shot the closest two mules in the back of the head right between their ears. They fell under the wheels and locked 'em up and we skidded about a half mile before I got the wagon stopped. By the time I got things back under control, those dead mules didn't hardly have a patch of skin left on 'em."

"That really worked, huh?"

"You bet it did, Marshal. I felt real bad about having to kill those mules 'cause they were fine, big ones and worth almost a hundred dollars apiece. But that was the only thing I could think of to do right then and damned if it didn't save my life and the other four mules."

Longarm was impressed. "You sound like the kind of man we are always looking for to pin on a United States marshal's badge."

"I do?"

"Sure! What you did in that emergency tells me that you are a man who can think and react well in an emergency."

"I believe I am," Yocum told him. "How good are you with that six-shooter on your hip?"

"I'm not the fastest or even the most accurate. But I can handle my own under fire."

"And you've had to kill a lot of men?"

Longarm's expression grew solemn. "Yes, I have."

"How many?"

"More than I care or even try to remember."

Yocum shook his head. "I don't know if I could stand killing a bunch of men . . . even if they deserved it. Not all outlaws are so terrible. Besides, I thought lawmen were supposed to arrest outlaws and bring them to trial."

"They are, but it often doesn't work out that way. Sometimes you just have to shoot the bad ones before they shoot you first."

"Have you been shot before?"

"Oh yes. And stabbed and beaten."

"You look like you got beat up," Yocum said, glancing at the purplish marks still on Longarm's face.

"I was in a bad fight."

"With Frank Brown," Yocum interrupted. "Yes, I knew that. Everyone in Central City knows what you did up there at Rivergold. Word of something that important travels like a wildfire. You're a hero up in the mining country."

"I don't feel like any hero," Longarm told the mule-skinner. "I just feel lucky to have survived. We knew Frank Brown as Mad Dog Trabert. He might well have used both names as an alias and so we'll never really know his true name. That doesn't matter. He was bad right down to his boots and deserved to die."

"We heard about what he did to those folks in the bank. Did you kill off the whole gang?"

"No," Longarm said. "There are two more to settle with up in Wyoming."

"Are you going after them?"

"Yep. Just as soon as I can get back on the train to Cheyenne."

"I sure would like to see it when you face them last two down."

"Are you serious about wanting to become a lawman?"

Longarm asked, changing the subject. "Because, if you are, I'll introduce you to my boss who will introduce you to his boss. After those interviews, you could be hired."

"It's that easy?" Yocum asked, looking surprised.

"No, it's not. First you have to be recommended by a marshal . . . and I'll do that. Then you have to pass both interviews, and they ask some tough questions."

"Such as?"

"How old are you?"

"That's easy," Yocum said, looking relieved.

"No," Longarm said, "I mean, how old are you?"

"Twenty-two."

"Good enough. Do you see that switchback just up ahead?"

"Sure."

"Pull over there and let's see how good you really are with a six-gun."

"You mean you want me to fire from this here wagon?"

"That's right. Will the mules panic?"

"No, sir. But . . ."

"If I'm going to recommend you, Dave, I have to be sure that you can do what you say you can do. Understand?"

"I understand, Marshal."

When Yocum pulled the wagon off the steep dirt road and set the brake, Longarm unholstered his gun and searched for a target. He spotted a little pine tree that was maybe thirty yards distant and no bigger around than his wrist. Pointing it out to the muleskinner he said, "Shoot that little pine standing just down the hill all by itself."

"You want me to draw and fire? I can do that without a holster. I draw from behind the waistband of my pants."

"No," Longarm said. "Just stand up, take quick aim and fire three times. If you hit it even once I'll consider that pretty fair shooting."

Yocum nodded and was grinning when he stood up. He

raised the gun and fired in rapid succession. He never missed.

"That's excellent," Longarm said. He pointed down to a Winchester rifle. "Now pick that one up and let's find you a tougher target."

"How about that white rock resting way down there all by itself?" Yocum asked.

"That would be a difficult shot. Downhill and a good distance."

"Shoot," Yocum said, "that's nothing much."

And the young man proved it by drilling the rock dead center and shattering it like a cube of ice.

"I'm satisfied," Longarm said. "Think it over on the rest of the way down to Denver and, if you're still of a mind to become a lawman, I'll vouch for you when we arrive at the federal office."

"I'm going to give it some real serious thought the rest of the trip," Yocum promised. "So, if I don't say much the rest of the way, you'll understand why."

"I sure will. But there's just one last thing I have to tell you, Dave."

"I'm all ears."

"It's a dangerous job. You often work alone and sometimes you have to buck long odds. You think that the local marshals will help you, but they can be your worst enemies. They get jealous and want to run the show, and you have to be firm and tell them that you're in charge and your authority overrides their authority. That's not what they want to hear. So you see, being a federal marshal is not only dangerous but it can be lonesome."

"I like my own company fine, but I do admit to being afraid of dying."

"We all are," Longarm told the muleskinner. "But we deal with that and most of us manage to survive until we're promoted into the office. Can you read and write?"

"Yes, sir. I've had book learning. I wasn't a real fine student, but I did passable."

"Good. Then think it over and tell me what you've decided when we get into the city."

When they drove down Larimer Street many hours later, Dave leaned over and said, "I've decided that I'd really like to become a marshal. And any good words you can put in for me would be appreciated."

Longarm was pleased. Dave Yocum wasn't the first young man he'd recommended to Billy Vail and he probably wouldn't be the last. But Yocum seemed to Longarm to be extremely well-suited for the work of carrying out the law, and he would give the muleskinner a great recommendation.

"I got to deliver this load of lumber, unhitch the mules and hand over some paperwork," Yocum told Longarm when he pulled his team to a halt just outside the federal building. "Then I can hurry on over . . . if that is all right with you."

"I'll be here waiting to introduce you to my boss," Longarm said, giving Yocum directions up to his office. "Then we'll see if we can get you hired on with the federal government."

"Would I get to wear a badge right away?"

"Yep."

"And would they send me out to hunt wanted men?"

"Not by yourself," Longarm told the man. "You'd be sent out with experienced lawmen the first year. Once you proved you can handle the responsibilities of a lawman, you'd be assigned the easier and less dangerous cases for another year. After that, if you're still on the payroll, you'd be expected to handle tough cases on your own."

"My, oh my!" Dave Yocum exclaimed. "Wouldn't momma be proud of her Oklahoma farm boy!"

Longarm appreciated Yocum's enthusiasm. Too bad

that some of the other men under Billy didn't share it. "What about your father?"

Yocum looked away for a moment. "Truth is," he finally admitted, "my pa was a stagecoach robber and he got gunned down last year trying to pull a holdup outside of Tucson, Arizona."

"Dave, why don't you not mention that part of your family history," Longarm suggested. "I know that it has nothing to do with you, but it certainly won't impress the people that you need to impress."

"I understand," Yocum said. "And I won't tell them about my older brother, either."

"Your older brother?"

Yocum expelled a deep sigh. "Yes, sir. Poor, dumb Mort used six sticks of dynamite to blow up a bank vault in Wichita, Kansas, but he wasn't standing back far enough and, when the smoke and dust cleared, they couldn't hardly find enough pieces left of him to fill a cigar box."

Longarm didn't hesitate to say, "You're right. Don't tell them about Mort or your father."

"I just want to be honest," Yocum said. "And I don't know if that means that I should tell them about my cousins who—"

"Stop!" Longarm frowned with growing exasperation. "Why don't you just not tell them about *any* of your relatives . . . except maybe your mother. She didn't rob or kill anyone, did she?"

"Naw. My ma, bless her soul, never hurt anyone except for . . ."

"Try to steer the conversation away from your family," Longarm blurted. "Tell them that you're a fine shot and muleskinner and that story about shooting the two mules to keep yourself and the other animals from flying off the side of the road over a cliff."

"I'll do that."

141

"Good." Longarm climbed down. "I'll see you in about an hour."

"I'll be here!" Yocum vowed, grinning from ear to ear with youthful optimism as he drove his team down the street.

Longarm watched the young man and his big wagon turn a corner and disappear. He didn't know what to think, given Yocum's notorious family background, but he figured that every man ought to be judged by his own merits.

Pushing that out of his mind, Longarm started up the stairs of the federal building. Billy was probably going to be upset at him for taking a full week off, but dammit, he needed the time to recover and . . . well, make sure that he was still fit.

Chapter 13

As soon as Longarm stepped into the federal building, Polly Raymond spotted him and came rushing up to his side. "Custis, what happened to your face and where have you been?"

"I got into a bad fight." He managed a tight smile though it still hurt. "Actually, I thought I looked pretty good by now compared to the shape my face was in a week ago."

"You still look terrible. Mr. Ludlow is furious and wants to see you right away."

"What's he upset about?"

"I don't know."

Longarm frowned. "I should probably stop by and visit Billy for a few minutes so that I know why I'm in trouble."

"Mr. Vail took off for Laramie three days ago."

"Billy went up to Laramie on his own after Jude and Mando Lopez?"

"No, Mr. Ludlow had him on the carpet and when the dust cleared, he sent both Mr. Vail and Deputy Marshal Avery."

Longarm groaned. "He sent George up with Billy?"

"That's right."

Longarm started back out the door but Polly grabbed his arm. "You can't just run up there without seeing Mr. Ludlow first!"

"Watch me," Longarm grated. There was a big clock on the lobby wall and Longarm glanced up at it and said, "The northbound train to Cheyenne leaves in less than an hour. I don't have time to see Mr. Ludlow."

"But if you run off without seeing him he'll fire you! Custis, please take a few minutes and go up and see him. It could mean your career."

"All right," Longarm reluctantly agreed. "But if he tells me to stay here or even tries to delay my catching the train, then I'll storm out of his office no matter what the consequences. Billy and George are no match for those two killers."

Longarm knew where Ludlow's office was located on the second floor. He had spoken to the man a few times but never really visited with him. Ludlow collected insects and was particularly proud of his butterfly collection. It was said to be his favorite topic of conversation.

For crying out loud, Longarm thought, *why would any self-respecting marshal want to carry on a conversation about that kind of nonsense?*

A few minutes later, Longarm received a cold, officious greeting by Mr. Ludlow's secretary, but he was ushered directly into the administrator's office. The man was working on papers and didn't even look up for a few moments, giving Longarm time to study his office. There were specimen boards mounted on the walls upon which were pinned a great variety of insects. Some were all of various beetles, two of just butterflies and several more were of grasshoppers and other insects whose names and origins Longarm did not even care to guess.

Their bureau administrator actually reminded Longarm of an insect. He was a tall man, dark and flinty-looking

144

with large, beetlish eyebrows and a long, narrow face. As he worked his pencil in fierce concentration, his eyebrows moved up and down like busy caterpillars and the corners of his thin and severe mouth curved downward. Ludlow had a pointed chin and deep-set eyes. His hands were so bony that the tendons were all visible across the back of his hand.

"Sit down," Ludlow commanded, finally glancing up but not bothering to rise from behind his desk and offer a civil greeting. "Marshal Long, where in the hell have you been the last five days?"

"Up in Central City recuperating from my injuries. I'm sure that Billy . . . I mean, Mr. Vail told you what happened when we finally caught up with Mad Dog Trabert."

"He did and I was very upset that I wasn't appraised of the entire investigation much earlier."

"You were on business in Washington, sir."

"True, but you could have telegraphed me," Ludlow snapped, clearly upset.

Longarm planted his feet wide apart and squared his broad shoulders. Free and unencumbered by family responsibilities, he knew that he could always find another good job, but Billy Vail was another matter. "If we'd have done that, the investigation might have become public knowledge and then we'd likely have been stonewalled. I take full responsibility for everything."

Longarm's words of contrition seemed to have a positive effect on the bureau administrator, who lowered his voice and said, "Marshal Long, do you realize the extreme importance of this case?"

"I do. It was one of the most brutal and cold-blooded executions I've ever seen in my entire career as a United States deputy marshal."

"That is quite correct," Ludlow said, dropping his pencil and coming to his feet. He went over to one of his insect boards and studied beetles for a moment. Then he returned to his chair. "It created an enormous backlash of anger and outrage in Denver. Our newspaper carried it as a front-page story for a full week. And can you imagine the kind of attention this case would receive if the press got ahold of it right now?"

"I do, and so did Billy . . . I mean, Mr. Vail. That's why we told no one and decided we had no choice but to act quickly and decisively."

"I suppose I understand."

"You do?"

"Yes. It is for those same reasons that I sent Marshal Vail and Deputy Marshal Avery up to Laramie to make the arrests of the last two members of the gang. I'm sure that they can handle the assignment and bring credit to themselves and to this office."

Longarm's eyes came to rest on Ludlow's desk ornament, which was a purple butterfly pinned to a piece of driftwood. The magnificent butterfly was huge with orange dots speckled across its wings. The creature appeared so alive that it seemed ready to take wing.

Longarm chose his next words very carefully because of their serious implications. "Sir, no offense to either of those men, but they're really not up to the job."

"What?"

"I have enormous respect for Billy, but he's been out of the field too long. And George Avery is completely incompetent."

Ludlow's busy eyebrows shot up. "Are you aware that he is my nephew?"

"Sure, and so is everyone else in this building," Longarm replied, his own anger starting to rise. "Why else would you have given George a badge?"

"How dare you speak about a fellow officer that way!"

"Mr. Ludlow, Billy Vail is a credit to your department and a fine man. For all I know, George Avery is also a fine man. But they are both in trouble and in way over

146

their heads against Jude and Mando Lopez."

"Marshal Long, I've heard just about enough of that for one day."

"If Billy and George are gunned down up in Laramie, sir, there will be a second tremendous public outcry. Everyone in Denver from the reporters to the mayor to the man on the street will demand to know why a kindly desk administrator and your nephew—who everyone in this building knows is a fool—were sent up to Laramie to be gunned down by two vicious bank robbers. And what are you going to tell them when that happens, Mr. Ludlow?"

Ludlow's cheeks puffed in and out and his mouth worked silently for a moment before he stammered, "Are you that sure those two will be killed in Laramie?"

"Yes," Longarm said, "I am. So sure that I'm willing to—"

"Excuse me!" Dave Yocum called, bursting past the secretary into Mr. Ludlow's office. "Don't mean to interrupt, but is this the head man I'm supposed to talk to before I can wear a marshal's badge?"

"Yeah," Longarm said, "but . . ."

Yocum ran across the office, grabbed Ludlow's bony hand and pumped it vigorously. "Sir, it will be a real honor to join your department and go after outlaws. I'll guarantee you that I'll bring 'em back dead or wishin' they was dead."

"Who the devil is this?" Ludlow cried, tearing his hand free and recoiling.

"Nice butterfly," Yocum said, grabbing up the little piece of driftwood and stroking the insect's wings.

"Put that down!" Ludlow thundered.

Yocum dropped the decoration and, unfortunately, it landed upside down. When Ludlow snatched it up, one of the insect's wings had fallen off and the other was shredded. Its head was missing too.

Ludlow's eyes widened in horror. "Do you realize what this . . ."

"I seen a lot of them little devils up by the pass. I can find you plenty, if you want to send me up there someday."

Ludlow was so flustered that he couldn't even respond so Longarm started talking. "Sir, I really need some assistance up in Laramie. This is Dave Yocum and he's first-rate with a gun or a rifle. I'd appreciate it, sir, if you'd deputize Mr. Yocum and put him on the payroll right now so we can catch that northbound train up to Cheyenne."

"What . . ."

"Dave Yocum," Longarm said, "will make a fine United States deputy marshal and I need him deputized now, sir."

Ludlow dropped the ruined butterfly decoration and turned his attention to the grinning young muleskinner. "Are you qualified for this job, young man?"

"Yes, sir. I've been around outlaws all my life!"

"He means," Longarm quickly added, "that he has fought lawlessness wherever he's found it and . . . and won the good fight."

"Hmmm," Ludlow said. "Are you prepared to risk your life up in Laramie?"

"Yes, sir!"

"All right then," Ludlow said, opening his desk drawer and finding a badge. "This seems to be an emergency. Pin this on and I'll swear you in as a United States deputy marshal."

"That's it?" Yocum asked, looking a trifle disappointed. "You don't want to hear about how I shot those mules and saved . . ."

"Not now," Longarm said. "Just . . . just be quiet and let Mr. Ludlow swear you in and then come down to my office and we'll get you outfitted with the basics."

"What basics?"

"A holster, for starters."

"Whatever you say, friend."

Dave Yocum was sworn in quickly and as they rushed out the door to catch the train, Ludlow shouted, "Which mountain pass?"

"I'll tell you later, Mr. Ludlow!" Yocum yelled as they hurried down the hallway. "Right now, we got a train and some killers to catch!"

They'd caught the train and ridden up to Cheyenne, where they'd caught the westbound that would take them over the Laramie Mountains into Laramie.

Longarm couldn't sit still that entire day it took to reach Laramie and when their train finally did pull into the railroad and ranching town, he was swinging off the coach even before it came to a complete stop.

"Hey!" Yocum shouted as they raced across the train platform and then up the street. "Slow down a little."

"No time. Come on!"

They ran up the street and it occurred to Longarm that he didn't exactly know where to start hunting for Billy and George. Most likely, they'd have checked into one of the town's better hotels. Billy was kind of picky about where he laid his head at night and he wasn't about to board in some filthy cow town flophouse.

"Let's try the Empire Hotel first," Longarm said, hurrying inside one of Laramie's better hotels. He rushed up to the registration desk. "I'm looking for a couple of men named Billy Vail and George Avery."

"And who might you be?" the desk clerk asked, looking bored and disinterested.

Longarm started to tell him but Yocum dragged out his new badge and shouted, "We're United States marshals and, from now on, *we'll* do the askin' and you'll do the answerin'. Got it?"

Yocum's overly assertive manner could have backfired and caused the desk clerk to bristle and be uncooperative but, fortunately, that didn't happen. In fact, the man dragged out the registration book and turned it around so that Longarm and Yocum could read the entries.

"It won't take you but a moment to see if they've been here," the clerk said nervously.

Longarm scanned the names. The Empire boasted almost thirty rooms and, with guests coming and going, there were two full pages of names to read, but none of them were the ones he sought.

"I guess they haven't been here," Longarm said.

They hurried outside and split up, Longarm directing Yocum to visit all the hotels on the south side of the street while he'd take those on the north side.

"We'll meet in a few minutes at the end of the block. With luck, we should find them pretty quick unless they've left town."

"Now why would they do that?" Yocum asked.

"I'll tell you later," Longarm replied. "Let's go!"

Longarm visited three more hotels and learned that Billy and George had not been among their guests. But when he met Yocum on the street corner in front of the Roundup Saloon, he could tell that his young friend had important news.

"I found 'em!" Yocum shouted, loud enough to be heard in far-off Cheyenne. "They stayed three nights in the Sheridan Hotel but they checked out just the day before yesterday."

"Did the desk clerk have any idea where they might have gone?"

"I don't know. Didn't ask." Yocum frowned. "I guess I should have, huh?"

"Yeah," Longarm said. "Let's go back to the Sheridan and see if we can get a lead."

"I sure hope they're still in town," Yocum said.

Longarm was taller than the former muleskinner and he was really covering ground. "I just hope they're still *alive*."

When they reached the Sheridan, Longarm strode swiftly across the old lobby with its scarred but polished wooden floor. There were the mounted heads of elk, buffalo, moose and even a grizzly bear hanging on the walls, all of them gazing down with glittering, glassy brown eyes.

"Excuse me," Longarm said to the desk clerk who was reading the newspaper. "I understand that you have had guests named Bill Vail and George Avery."

The clerk was bald and dapper with a white silk handkerchief stuffed into his coat pocket. He wore a monocle and was smoking a slender black cigar. Looking up from his paper with a disapproving expression, he said, "That's right. I told your loud young friend that they were registered here."

"When?"

The clerk sighed as if he had been greatly inconvenienced. He stood up and found the register book behind the counter, then hauled it out and opened up the pages and ran his finger down the entries until he came to Bill Vail's name.

"There," he said stepping back and folding his arms across his narrow chest. "Read it for yourself."

Longarm took in the entry at a glance and saw that it was just as Yocum had explained. Billy had registered himself and George Avery for three nights and they'd checked out three days ago.

"Do you know where they went?" Longarm asked.

"Of course not," the hotel clerk said, removing his monocle and glaring at Longarm. "That is none of our business."

"I know." Longarm resented the man's arrogance and was trying his damnedest not to reach across the counter and throttle this irritating little man. "But they might have mentioned in passing where they were headed."

"No, they did not."

"Think harder, you little fart!" Yocum shouted, sending the clerk reeling backward.

"Really!" the clerk exclaimed after bouncing off the back wall. "I won't stand being spoken to in that tone of voice."

Before Longarm could grab the newly appointed young marshal, Yocum was flying around the counter and grabbing the clerk by his shirt front. Hauling the squirming and now-terrified man up on his toes, Yocum shouted in his face. "Ya musta heard something, you snotty little pipsqueak. Now talk or I'll bust your ugly little beak!"

"I . . . I overhead them saying they had to rent horses and go after some men. They . . . they said they were going north along the Laramie Mountains to discover some isolated ranch."

"What ranch?" Yocum hissed.

"They didn't say! Please let me down."

"Marshal Yocum, put the man down," Longarm ordered.

"I ain't sure he's remembered everything yet. Have you, little man?"

"Yes. I swear I have!"

"Let him down," Longarm repeated, making a mental note to explain to the ex-muleskinner that lawmen were not supposed to intimidate or rough up innocent witnesses.

Yocum released the clerk but not before saying, "Where would Marshals Vail and Avery rent saddle horses in this town?"

"Maybe the Western Livery. Or the Bateman Livery. Those are the two biggest and closest." The desk clerk swallowed hard, looking pale and faint. "They're just up the street, Marshal!"

"Let's go," Longarm said, heading for the door.

"Thanks for remembering to remember," Yocum called back over his shoulder.

"You . . . you big bruiser! You smell like . . . like a dirty old mule!"

Yocum barked a laugh as they hurried down the street toward the liveries.

"Did I do good?" the young marshal asked.

"You did fine," Longarm said. "Sometimes, though, it helps to use a little more diplomacy."

"What?"

"Never mind. You got the information we needed and, right now, that's all that is important."

"You bet," Yocum said. "And, if the fellas that own these livery stables have trouble remembering . . . I'll help them out too!"

Longarm said nothing but he couldn't resist a thin smile. Dave Yocum was rough as a cob and ignorant of law, but he had the talent and enthusiasm to be one hell of a fine marshal . . . if he didn't get killed or fired first.

Chapter 14

"Are you Mr. Bateman?" Longarm asked an old man who was currying a horse at the Bateman Livery.

The man turned and studied Longarm and Yocum. "Now that sort of depends who's asking. If you're after my money, I'm Joe Smith."

"We're not after your money," Longarm said, showing the man his badge. "I'm Marshal Long and this is Marshal Yocum. We're looking for two other marshals that left town three days ago on rented horses. I'm hoping they rented those mounts from you."

"They did," Bateman said. "Along with saddles and gear they'd need to be out for a week. They bought food and ammunition and lit out of here last . . . let's see. Wednesday. Yes. Three days ago. Anything happen to my horses?"

"Not that I know of," Longarm replied. "But those two men could be riding into more trouble than they're prepared to handle."

"They didn't seem too tough to me, either," Bateman said. "But I didn't ask why they were in such a hurry to leave and they didn't volunteer any information. What's going on?"

"We need to go find and help them," Longarm said. "To do that we also need to rent a pair of horses, food and supplies."

"I got plenty of good saddle horses. Cost you one dollar a day per animal. I'll expect you to bring them back in good shape and, to do that, you'll need to pack some grain."

"Fair enough."

"The blacksmith just tacked shoes on a pair of my best horses. Want to take a look?"

"Sure," Longarm said. "Where'd the other two marshals say they were going?"

Bateman shrugged. "They didn't actually seem to know themselves."

"What does that mean?"

"It means that they asked me a lot of questions about the country and the rivers up to the north along the western slope of the Laramies. And they wanted to know if I'd ever heard of the J-Bar outfit."

"The J-Bar?" Yocum asked.

"Yeah. It's an old outfit that changed names about five years ago. Used to be the Rocking T, but a fella named Jude Slaney bought the ranch and changed it to the J-Bar."

Longarm glanced at Yocum, then back at the livery owner and asked, "What can you tell me about Jude Slaney?"

"Not much. He only comes into town about every other month. He's not friendly. He has no family and drinks pretty heavy on the nights that he stays over in town. Slaney likes the saloon ladies and I've heard he pays them well for their services. The man has five or six cowboys on his payroll and they don't get to Laramie very often either."

"Is one of his hands a Mexican named Mando Lopez?"

"That's right. Why do you ask?"

"We need to talk to them," Longarm said.

"So did the two marshals that rented from me on Wednesday."

"Is that right?"

"Yeah," Bateman said, "and I'll tell you the same thing I told them. The J-Bar bunch is tough. They've got such a bad reputation up north that some of their neighboring ranchers are considering an all-out range war."

"Why is that?" Yocum asked.

"Seems that Slaney and his boys are pretty slick with a rope and a running iron. They're branding everything that they can lay their hands on and they don't care who knows it. Last year Mando Lopez gunned down a cowboy from the Double-O Ranch who accused him of rustling. There's a lot of bad blood up there in that high country."

"What does Lopez look like?"

"He's tall for a Mexican. Maybe thirty years old and a fancy dresser. Wears a sombrero, silk bandanas and rides a handsome black stallion. He always wears those big-roweled Mexican spurs made of solid silver with jingle bobs that you can hear even when he's on horseback. Someone once made the mistake of calling him a cowboy. Lopez got real indignant and insisted he was a *vaquero*! He made quite a stink about that, and it sure didn't go over well with the cowboys in this part of the country."

"What does Jude Slaney look like?" Longarm asked.

"He's a big man like yourself with bright red hair and lots of freckles. He has long front teeth . . . bucktoothed is what he is and he reminds me of a huge rabbit. But you'd never want to say that to his face because he has a bad temper. When Jude Slaney gets drunk, people clear out of the saloon and wait until he passes out on the floor."

"He's our man," Longarm said to Yocum. "There's no doubt about it now."

"Mr. Bateman, how quick can you have them horses ready for us?" Yocum asked.

"Just as soon as you can get your supplies. I'd suggest you buy your supplies over at Hank's Merchantile and Grocery."

"We'll be ready to leave in thirty minutes," Longarm decided.

Bateman nodded. "Boys, if you cross onto the J-Bar Ranch, you'd better be prepared to run or fight."

"We'll fight," Longarm vowed, his expression grim as he wondered what might have become of Billy Vail and George Avery.

They rode all that morning and afternoon, flanking the snowcapped Laramie Mountains while fording ice-cold rivers and streams. This was fine cattle country, with dozens of small ranches dotting the western foothills. The day had started out with blue skies, but dark clouds were forming and thunderheads were gathering on the nearest peaks.

"If I didn't want to be a lawman," Yocum said as they traversed a wide, grassy valley ringed with big pines, "I'd want to be a cattleman and have a little outfit resting up against those pretty mountains."

"It would be nice," Longarm agreed. "But the snows can get pretty deep up in this country and the winter winds are cold."

Yocum just shrugged. "I'm tough. If you're going to make it as a muleskinner, you had better be tough or you won't last."

"I expect that's the truth," Longarm replied. In a few hours, the sun would set. He was pretty sure that it was going to rain, and they needed to find shelter before long and start thinking about exactly where the J-Bar was to be found. "Dave, there's a ranch up ahead. I think we ought to stop there and get some directions and maybe even a barn to hole up in when the sky opens up tonight."

"Sounds good to me," Yocum replied. "Maybe there's some pretty young ranch girl living there that will take a shine to me now that I'm a genuine United States marshal. Say, how come you don't wear your badge like I'm doing?"

"Glad you brought that up," Longarm told his friend. "Someone will complain now and then that a marshal should wear his badge out in the open. But that can be a fatal mistake."

"How come?"

"If you live long enough hunting down outlaws," Longarm said, "you'll learn that some of them like to shoot first and ask questions later. I once knew a marshal who walked into a saloon wearing his badge and he was shot dead by someone he'd arrested and sent to prison several years earlier. The poor fella didn't have a chance."

Yocum studied Longarm closely. "I suppose you've made more than your share of enemies."

Longarm dipped his chin in agreement. "If you're taking your work seriously, you'll make a lot of arrests. You'll send the worst to the gallows, others to jail and some to federal prisons. And those that go to jail or prison will *never* forget what you did to them even though they deserved their sentences."

"I see."

"And that's only the half of it," Longarm continued. "Every man you arrest or kill has family. And you can be sure that some of them will hate you forever. So you might walk into a store or be riding up the road and one of those family members will see your badge and decide right then and there to seek revenge and get even. And the worst part of it is . . . you've probably never seen them before so you don't have a chance."

"Geez," Yocum said, shaking his head. "I never thought so many people would want my scalp."

"They don't yet," Longarm told the young man, "but if you stay on the job long enough they will."

Yocum removed the shiny badge he'd worn so proudly and slipped it into his shirt pocket. He rode along in silence for a few minutes and then said, "The way you talk, a federal marshal is a marked man. A loner living on borrowed time."

"I don't look at it that way," Longarm replied. "We just have a tough but necessary job to do. And there are a lot of benefits."

"Such as?

"Well," Longarm began, "can you imagine what this country would be like if no one had the guts to enforce the law?"

"Not good."

"Far, far worse than that," Longarm said. "It would be every man for himself and the strongest would either kill or run off the weakest. It would be the law of the gun. That's the way it used to be out here on the frontier. And there are still some who miss those times. They're the men that took what they wanted from others and then laughed in their faces."

"Outlaws like some that I have in my own family."

"That's right, and they respect nothing but force. They have no moral code, no sense of decency or interest in what is wrong or right. They just take what they want when they want it. I expect that Jude Slaney, Mando Lopez and the others that are on the J-Bar payroll all share that criminal mentality."

"You're probably right," Jude said, "but I was brought up to believe that you had to be quick with your fists or a gun and strong or you'd never get anywhere in life."

"I'm not suggesting that weakness is a virtue," Longarm said. "I'm saying that might doesn't make right."

"It did where I grew up. In school, a fella either stood up and fought or he got run off with his tail between his legs. There wasn't anything worse than being branded a chicken or a coward."

"I understand that. And it wasn't any different when I was a boy in West Virginia. But I remember one kid named Arthur Hamilton. He was smaller than the rest of us and just plain sickly. His nose was always running. He whined and was a real sissy. The kids picked on him just like chickens will always pick at the weakest bird in the flock."

Longarm lapsed into silence.

"Well, what happened to Arthur?" Yocum asked.

"One day he made the mistake of bringing a real nice pocketknife to school. It was his late father's knife and his mother had given it to him for his twelfth birthday. It was a fine knife and when the other bigger boys saw it, they took it away from Arthur. When he started to cry, they taunted him. I asked the bigger kids to give the knife back but they laughed in my face and dared me to try and get it back for Arthur. They were older and bigger and I was afraid so I walked away."

"And poor crybaby Arthur lost the knife?"

"No, the teacher learned about it and made them give the knife back to Arthur. But it was too late."

"What do you mean 'it was too late?' "

"This big bully named Hob Porter had stuck the knife blade between the cracks of the schoolhouse floor and then snapped it off. He did it out of pure spite and meanness. So when Arthur got his knife back, it was ruined."

"That was an awful thing to do," Yocum said.

"Yes, it was. But you know what?"

"What?"

"Arthur got something else that had belonged to his dead pa . . . an old skinning knife. And the very next day he sneaked up behind Hob Porter and drove the blade between his shoulders right up to the hilt. Hob died screaming after about an hour. The long-bladed skinning

161

knife had pierced his lung and who knows what else deep inside."

Yocum shook his head. "So what happened to Arthur?"

"He was arrested and sent off to some place up in Charleston for real bad kids. I never saw Arthur again. But I heard he grew up mean and knifed two more bullies to death before he was hanged at the age of twenty-one."

"I guess he got what was coming to him," Yocum said after a period of thoughtful silence.

"I guess," Longarm agreed. "But I've often wondered if I'd been big enough to whip Hob Porter and protect Arthur, if four men wouldn't be alive today."

"The three that Arthur stabbed to death and himself before he was hanged on the gallows?"

"That's right."

"But maybe Hob deserved to die and so did the other two that Arthur stabbed."

"Maybe. But maybe they were made bullies by other, bigger bullies. And maybe if there had been some kind of law or justice in their childhoods, the whole thing would never have happened."

Yocum dipped his chin and silently chewed on that for a while as thunder rolled over the Laramies and lightning played with the jagged peaks. The temperature was dropping, and a cold wind began to blow. No doubt about it, they were going to get wet this night and Longarm just hoped they wouldn't get caught in an early snow.

When they grew nearer to the ranch house, Yocum finally said, "Custis, maybe you're trying to make up for what you felt you should have done in the school yard back in West Virginia."

"There's some truth there," Longarm admitted. "All I know is that I hate bullies. And all outlaws are bullies. They prey on the weak. Kill them. Beat them. Rob them. Turn them into hate-filled Arthurs. You figure it out for yourself."

162

Yocum nodded, and a few minutes later Longarm hailed the ranch house, which was a huge and rambling log cabin nestled up beside the tall pines. It had a big front porch, three or four outbuildings and a nice hay barn.

"Someone sure has a nice spread here," Yocum said. "But I don't see their cattle."

"Maybe Jude Slaney and his men have cleaned them all out," Longarm said.

"You might be right about that," Yocum agreed.

The doorway to the cabin opened and an old man wearing faded bib overalls appeared with a gun in one hand and a crutch in the other. "What do you want?" he demanded.

Longarm saw a rifle poking ever so slightly through a window. It was dim inside the cabin so he couldn't see who or how many people were there, but he could almost smell their fear.

"We're United States marshals," he said.

"Let me see your badges," the shaky old man replied. "Reach for them with your left hands and do it real slow and easy."

"Mister, what is wrong with you?" Yocum asked, clearly puzzled by this reception. "We . . ."

"Just do as he asks and we'll be fine," Longarm told his partner as he retrieved his badge.

"Now you," the old man ordered, gun moving toward Yocum.

The young marshal did what he'd been ordered and when they were both holding their badges out in plain view, the rancher hobbled out on his crutch and insisted on taking a closer look. Finally satisfied, he said, "All right," and shoved his pistol into his bib overall pocket. "What can I do for you good men today?"

"We're looking for the J-Bar Ranch," Longarm said. "I understand it's somewhere in this neck of the woods."

At the mention of the J-Bar, the old man stiffened and his face grew as dark as the storm clouds overhead. "It's because of that outfit that I spoke to you so unfriendly! Jude Slaney has rustled every last one of my cattle, and his men ambushed me out by the lake and shattered my right ankle with a rifle's bullet. They ran off my three cowboys. I can't ride and I can't work anymore. What am I going to do? I got daughters to feed and clothe!"

"Did you see who actually fired the shot?" Yocum asked.

"No," the rancher swore bitterly. "But I know it was either Slaney or one of them others. They're all cut from the same rotten cloth. They want my land and . . . and they want my girls."

"Pa?"

Longarm and Yocum turned their attention to the doorway.

"You girls can put the rifles down and come out," the old man said, his voice hoarse and thick with emotion. "These two fellas are lawmen. We got nothing to fear from 'em."

The old man's daughters were tall, slender and lovely. The younger one might have been fifteen and the older one perhaps twenty. They were brown eyed and both carried rifles, which they now leaned up against the wall of the cabin.

Yocum swept off his hat. Eyes on the older girl, he introduced himself and Longram with more eloquence than would have been expected from a former muleskinner. He ended by saying, "We've come to get rid of the bullies that have been badgerin' you and your family."

"My name is Eloise Hastings," the older girl said, stepping out to extend her hand up to Yocum as cold raindrops started to pelt their faces. "And you are welcome to come inside and share what we have to eat . . . though it's not much. I shot a deer last week but it's mostly gone."

164

"That's mighty kind of you, Miss Eloise," Yocum said, looking to Longarm for approval.

The girl added, "You can put your horses in the corral, pitch them hay and then leave your saddles and gear in the hay barn."

"Thanks," Longarm told her.

"Miss, we have our own vittles and we'd be happy to share them with you," Yocum said, "if my friend agrees."

The rain began to fall harder and thunder boomed over the Laramie Mountains. Longarm dismounted saying, "We've flour and some things that we'll add to your larder."

"My name is Ben Hastings," the rancher said. "I'd help you out there but I can't get around very well anymore."

"We'll do fine," Longarm said, already leading his horse toward the barn. Yocum was lagging behind, talking to Eloise.

Longarm unsaddled quickly and had to yell at his friend to do the same thing before he was thoroughly soaked. After their saddles and gear were stowed in the dry shed and their horses were in the corral, Longarm grabbed some of their food and ran for the house in a cold downpour. Yocum was right on his heels.

"You got a fine ranch house," Yocum said after they'd removed their hats and coats. "Nice flooring and a handsome rock fireplace. We're much obliged to be out of the rain and we won't put you out any."

Eloise beamed and her younger sister, whose name was Annie, giggled.

"Have a seat by the fire and dry off," Ben Hastings said, indicating two empty chairs that had been brought over from the little area that served as a kitchen. "It's going to be a bad night."

"Mr. Hastings, you're mighty kind to invite us in for supper," Longarm told the man.

"You can sleep out in the bunkhouse or maybe even

throw your bedrolls on the floor in front of the fire where it'd be warmer tonight. There's plenty of room now that all our help has been run off by Jude Slaney."

"We're looking for two men that came up about three days ago on horseback from Laramie."

"There haven't been any riders passing by that I've seen." The rancher glanced over at his daughters. "Have you girls seen any riders?"

Both Eloise and Annie shook their heads.

Longram frowned, not knowing what to think. "They were United States marshals."

"What's going on?" Hastings asked.

"I'd rather not say, but it does have something to do with Jude Slaney."

"Doesn't surprise me a bit." The old man snorted. "I'll bet that you've found brands altered on cattle being shipped out of Laramie. Isn't that right?"

"We can look into that," Yocum said eagerly.

"I hope you do. I'm practically bankrupted because of the J-Bar. I went down to see the local constable in Laramie and he told me that since we were out of his jurisdiction he couldn't help us. But you know what I think?"

"No," Longarm said.

"I think he was just plain afraid to stand up to Jude Slaney and his men!" Hastings picked up a corncob pipe and angrily chewed on its stem. "Hell, I guess I can't really blame him. Slaney would have killed him for sure if he started poking his nose into what is happening up here."

"How far is it from here to the J-Bar Ranch?"

"Ten miles. Keep following the road north and when you top a red and rocky ridge, you'll look down on a big valley. That's the J-Bar. Once you start down into that valley you're fair game for Slaney and his men."

"Where is the ranch house in relationship to his valley?"

Hastings lit his pipe and sucked wetly on old tobacco. "You got something in mind for 'em?"

"I don't know yet," Longarm admitted. "But we might have to sneak up on them in order to get close enough to see what is going on."

"The J-Bar ranch house is set sorta back against the pines at the eastern side of the valley, just like my place sits back in this valley."

"Then we could probably manage to flank the valley and drop down behind the ranch house."

"You could try but I'm sure that Slaney has watchdogs. They'd most likely see you and set off the alarm."

"Thanks for the warning," Longarm said, glancing over at his deputy to see if he had any comments.

But Dave Yocum and Eloise Hastings were lost in each other's eyes and Annie had started cooking. Longarm jabbed the young deputy in the ribs and said, "We should turn in as soon as we eat."

"You go on ahead," Yocum told him.

Longarm sighed. He wasn't a bit sure anymore if Yocum was really cut out to be a loner like himself.

"What happened to your face?" Hastings asked.

"Got in a fight up in a place called Rivergold. It's just northwest of Central City in Colorado."

"I've heard of it. Boom town, huh?"

"Yeah."

"Must have been quite a fight."

"It was," Longarm said, not wishing to elaborate, although the urge was there to tell Hastings that his problems with Jude Slaney and his men were coming to an abrupt end.

"What do you think happened to your deputy friends?" Hastings asked.

"I don't know, but I am worried."

"I wish I could come along and help you hunt for them

but my ankle won't stand for being put in a stirrup. Maybe Eloise—"

"No," Longarm said, a little too quickly. "We'll be fine. What are you going to do without cattle?"

"I have no idea," the rancher told him. "If I buy more, then I'll lose 'em all to Slaney and his rustlers. If I *don't* buy more, then I have no reason for being here. This is good cattle country. There's a pretty big stand of timber on this spread but I won't log it off. I'd rather sell out."

"I wouldn't expect you could get much given your neighbor problem," Longarm said.

"You got that pegged right," Hastings told him. "And there are others like me in the same sad situation. You know what I think?"

"No."

Hastings jabbed the stem of his corncob at Longarm. "I think Slaney intends to starve us out and take over our abandoned ranches. I think he's let it be known from Cheyenne down to Denver that any new buyers up here will face the same situation that the current ranchers are facing."

"So you're stumped."

"I am unless you mean to arrest and imprison Jude Slaney and his bunch. Do you?"

Longarm drew a soggy cigar from his shirt pocket and lit it, taking time to chose his words carefully. "Mr. Hastings," he said at last, "I think that we are going to solve your bad neighbor problem real quick."

The old man beamed. "Amen!"

Yocum and Eloise, startled by the outcry, looked over with surprise, but Longarm said nothing. He was content to smell whatever Annie had begun to cook and to see a bright glimmer of hope appear in Ben Hasting's eyes.

Chapter 15

The sun was shining early the next morning when Long-arm left the bunkhouse and walked across the ranch yard to the house. Old man Hastings was already up and enjoying his pipe and a cup of coffee. When Longarm yawned and stretched, the rancher said, "Go on inside. There's a pot of coffee on the stove. The girls will soon be fixin' some breakfast. That is, if I can get Eloise up and moving."

"She sleeps in?"

"No, but her and Deputy Yocum took quite a shine to each other last evening. They sat out here on the porch together and watched it storm until the wee hours of the morning."

"Yocum is young and he bears watching," Longarm said going into the house. He returned a few minutes later with a steaming cup of coffee in his hand and took a rocking chair beside the rancher. "Fine morning."

"It is fine," Hastings agreed. "I sure would hate to give up this ranch. Me and my wife came here when there was nothing. We built this place together, raised both girls and enjoyed a pretty good life."

"When did your wife pass away?"

169

"Three years ago next month," Hastings said, pain leaping into his eyes. "She got a tumor in her and didn't last too long. Died hard, I'm afraid, and there isn't a day that I don't wish it was me that passed on instead of Mildred."

Longarm could see that the old rancher was serious. "At least you have the girls and this fine cattle ranch."

"For now," Hastings said. "One of these days, some young fella will ask me if he can have my permission to marry Eloise, then the same will happen with Annie. I just hope they're as good as Yocum."

"He is a good man."

"I heard him tell Eloise that he'd been a muleskinner up until last week."

"That's right. He grew up on a farm or a ranch, I forget which. He's a handy fella."

"Can he shoot straight?"

"He can," Longarm said.

"Does he know that he could get killed today?"

"I'm sure that he does."

"Then he's got some grit in his craw. I sure hope that you and Yocum can do whatever it is you're about to try."

"Me too."

"I was thinking," Hastings said, taking a sip of his coffee and staring out across his yard, "if you hitch up my buckboard, I could go along with you. I can still handle a shotgun and—"

"I don't think that would be a very good idea," Longarm interrupted.

"You need a *decoy*," the old man explained. "Someone comin' up the main road toward the ranch to attract the attention of the J-Bar cowboys and dogs. Otherwise, you won't even get close to the ranch house. And you want to see if your friends are either dead or alive there, don't you?"

"You're a pretty smart fella, Mr. Hastings. How did

you know that I am worried they might have been killed or taken prisoner?"

"I could tell," the rancher replied. "And that's why I think you ought to let me drive a buckboard up to the J-Bar ranch house and cause a commotion."

Longarm sipped his coffee and gave the matter some thought. He looked over at Hastings and said, "What if they shoot you before I can stop them?"

"I have a sawed-off shotgun and I'll hide it under a blanket next to me on the seat. If they draw guns, I'll open fire."

"And get yourself killed."

"Marshal, I'm a sick and heartbroken old man. My wife is gone and I've little stomach for life anymore. If it wasn't for Eloise and Annie, I'd just as soon be dead. I'm in constant pain from the bullet that shattered my ankle. I can't work, can't walk and . . . well, I can't do much of anything useful. So, if I can help you wipe out the scourge of this country, then I'll be more than happy to do it!"

"And if you died, what would become of your daughters?"

"I've taken the steps to see that they'll be fine. They can stay here and hire more cowboys after Slaney and I are gone . . . or they can sell out once the J-Bar is run out of business. Either way is better than the slow ruin we're now facing."

"I dunno," Longarm hedged.

"I'm beggin' you, Marshal Long. I've lived a full life. There's nothing left for me but the privilege of an honorable death. Killing Slaney, Lopez or any others among that bunch would be more than honorable." Hastings gave a dry chuckle. "If I could do that, then the good, hard-working people of this country would probably commission a bronze statue in my honor."

Longarm could see that Ben Hastings was dead serious. He could also see how a diversion would prove very helpful in getting up to the ranch house. It would mean the difference between success or failure, life or death.

"If I agree," Longarm finally said, "you'd have to do it my way . . . not your own."

"I understand."

"My way is to arrest Jude Slaney and Mando Lopez."

"On what charge? They've all been rustling cattle."

"On the charge of murder," Longarm said.

Hastings smiled. "I'd like that just fine. I'll do whatever you want, Marshal. But we have to tell my girls that all I'm going to do is to lead you up to that red rock ridge and wait to see that it goes well. Otherwise, they wouldn't stand for my leaving."

"Fair enough."

"Is young Yocum married?"

"Not that I know of."

"You think he's a hard worker and an honest man?"

"Yes, and I have high hopes that he'll become a fine lawman."

"Maybe he'd rather be a cattleman," Hastings said with a wink.

Longarm had to smile. "If we pull through this today, I expect that's a question you and Eloise might like to ask him."

"Yes," the rancher said, puffing rapidly on his pipe. "I expect it is."

They left the Hastings Ranch with the old man driving his buckboard while Longarm and Yocum rode alongside.

"You be real careful!" Eloise called as they left the ranch yard.

"We will," her father answered.

"You too, David!"

Longarm glanced over at his friend. Yocum had a silly grin on his face and that was troubling. "Are you going to be ready for whatever trouble we face today?"

"Hell yes!" Dave swore, snapping out of his romantic reverie.

"Then start thinking about Slaney and his bunch more and about Miss Hastings a whole lot less," Longarm ordered.

Yocum blushed with either anger or embarrassment. He raised his chin defiantly. "Custis, don't you worry yourself none. I'll be there when the trouble starts and I'll still be standing when the last shot is fired."

"Maybe we'll get lucky, catch the whole bunch by surprise and get the drop on them while Mr. Hastings has their full attention."

"Mr. Hastings," Yocum asked, "have you figured out what you're going to say to get their attention?"

"I'm going to tell them that I am sick and tired of their rustling my cattle. Then I'll threaten them some."

"But not too much," Longarm warned. "And give us about an hour to circle around behind the ranch house and get in position."

"I'll do that."

When the road finally lifted to the high, red rock ridge that the old man had described, Longarm said, "Can we see the J-Bar Ranch from just up ahead?"

"Yep."

"Then stay here and give us an hour."

"Is that going to be enough time, Marshal?"

Longarm dismounted and handed his reins to Yocum. "Hold my horse while I take a look at the layout of Slaney's ranch."

Longarm hiked a few hundred yards up to the broken ridge and peered down into the valley which was dotted by grazing cattle and horses. He could see the ranch house itself nestled among the pines that flanked the valley. The ranch and the valley were even bigger than he'd expected.

"Make that an hour and a half," Longarm said when he returned.

173

Ben Hastings dragged out his pocket watch. "My time-piece says it is nine-thirty."

Longarm looked at his Ingersol pocket watch. "Close enough. Drive over the top of the ridge at eleven o'clock. It will take you at least fifteen minutes to reach the ranch house. By then, they'll have spotted you and the wagon and we'll have come in close on foot."

"Good luck," Hastings said in farewell. "And no matter what happens . . . kill Jude Slaney. He's the one that is behind all our troubles. If you get him, the others won't know what to do and might even surrender."

"We'll see," Longarm replied.

"And David?" the rancher said.

"Yes, sir?"

"If the bullets start flying, don't be ashamed to duck."

"I won't."

Longarm and Yocum left the old man and reined off to the north. They'd flank the ranch and make their move while Ben Hastings waited to become their decoy. If all went as planned, perhaps this dangerous business could be taken care of without a shot being fired.

But Longarm doubted it.

Chapter 16

Everything went according to plan until they stumbled across Billy Vail and George Avery all shot to hell and hiding in a cave. Longarm and Yocum might have ridden right past the two marshals, except that Billy was still conscious and managed to toss a pebble downhill, which rolled under Longarm's horse causing it to jump. When he glanced up the mountainside, Longarm saw a hand weakly flutter into view.

"What the . . ."

"Custis!" Billy croaked from inside the cave. "Don't shoot!"

Longarm was off his horse and racing to his friend's side in an instant. When he ducked under the rock overhang and pushed back into the darkness of the little cave he dropped to his knees beside Billy. "What happened?"

"We rode up to Slaney's ranch house and tried to pretend we were just drifters looking for work. But they saw through that real quick. Especially after they asked us a few questions about cattle. We were outgunned so bad I knew they wouldn't surrender so I tried to rein my horse around and ride away."

"But they wouldn't let you."

"No," Billy said. "Jude got suspicious. They told us to dismount.

"I knew if we did that we were goners. I went for my gun and George went for his gun. We opened fire and . . . for a minute there . . . everything went crazy. Then I yelled for George to retreat and make a run for it. I was hit and so was he. We got away but I knew we couldn't ride far because George was hit bad. So we came up the mountain here."

Billy took a deep, ragged breath. He licked his lips and asked, "You got any water?"

"Dave! Bring our canteens!"

"Anyway," Billy said. "We lost them in these thick trees, but we were both too badly wounded to ride very far so we dismounted. I whipped our horses and they must have galloped ten miles. Jude Slaney and his bunch never found us because I brushed out our tracks. But they damn sure tried. Tried for a whole day."

Longarm tried to penetrate the darkness and he thought he saw a body farther back in the narrow cave. "Is that George?"

"Yeah. He's dead." Billy's voice cracked. "But he killed one of Slaney's gang before he took a bullet. We both emptied our guns before we turned tail. George turned out to be a brave man."

"I'm glad to hear that," Longarm said as Yocum joined them with the canteens. Longarm uncapped one of them and helped Billy drink. "Take it easy," he warned.

Billy slowed and finally lay back. "Who is that?" he asked, looking at the young marshal.

"Billy, meet Dave Yocum. He was deputized by Mr. Ludlow just a few days ago up in the man's office. I told Ludlow that I needed help and that Yocum was a man good with a gun."

"I hope you are," Billy said. "Anyway, I'm glad you're here to help."

"Thanks," Yocum replied.

"Are you hit bad?"

"When George and I bailed off our running horses I broke my arm. That and the bullet I took in the shoulder has got me feeling a bit out of sorts."

"You need a doctor," Longarm said. "But we've got an old rancher driving a buckboard into the J-Bar right now and I can't let him face Jude and his boys alone."

"We killed Mando Lopez and one other man," Billy said, easing himself into a sitting position. "I tried to kill Slaney but he was too quick. I got Lopez instead and George dropped another of them."

"You did fine," Longarm said. "All you have to do is hang on for a little while longer and then this will all be over. There must be a doctor in Laramie and we'll get you to him sometime tonight."

"I'm not staying in this cave with George any longer," Billy announced in a voice that brooked no argument. "I can still walk and hold a gun in my right hand. I'm coming with you."

Longarm scowled. "Are you sure?"

"Custis, besides Jude Slaney, there's at least five or six men at the J-Bar ranch and they all look like hard cases."

Longarm eased out of the little cave and checked his pocket watch. Watching him, Yocum asked, "What time is it?"

"Ten-thirty," he said. "Ben Hastings will be starting over the hill and down the road into that valley. We've no time to lose."

"Then let's go," Billy said.

Longarm helped Billy to his feet. "I wish you'd just stay here and watch over the horses."

"I can't do that. If you and Dave here are killed, I'd be in a bad fix. So you see, I'm going with you for my own selfish reasons."

"Sure," Longarm said, not believing a word of it.

Billy gulped more water and when he looked strong enough to walk, Longarm said, "Like it or not, you're going to take a position with my rifle in the trees and cover us."

"I outrank you," Billy grimly reminded him.

"I don't give a damn. For you it's either my way ... or no way. Follow my orders or I'll knock you down and tie you up. So what's it to be?"

"Okay. I'll give you cover fire from the trees," Billy agreed. "Let's go."

Longarm needed no urging. The few minutes that this delay had caused might prove very costly, especially for Ben Hastings.

The deadfall was thick and the pines grew close together. But somehow, they made it to a good viewpoint about fifty yards behind the ranch house. By then, Billy was trembling with exhaustion.

"I could use more water," he said.

Longarm gave him Dave's canteen, then positioned him behind a fallen log saying, "We're going to try and get the drop on them and take Jude and his boys alive. But you know what to do if they go for their guns."

"Damn right I do! I got a bullet in my shoulder and a dead deputy marshal lying back in that cave." Billy took a drink and then doused his handkerchief. He used it to wipe the perspiration from his brow. "Just don't take any chances. Not like George and I did a couple of days ago."

"We won't." Longarm looked to Yocum and then out to the valley where he could see the old rancher in his buckboard driving up the road.

"When the dogs start barking at Hastings, we'll run down to that barn and then on to the house."

Yocum drew his gun. "I'm ready."

Longarm waited, and soon three huge mongrels saw the buckboard and came charging out from the front of the

178

ranch house to challenge the arrival of old man Hastings. A few moments later, Longarm saw men pour out of the ranch house to intercept their angry neighbor.

"Let's go!" Longarm whispered.

They ran down the hill desperately trying to keep their footing on a slick and deep bed of pine needles. Longarm and Yocum both took a tumble but weren't noticed as Slaney and his men began a shouting match with Hastings. Longarm couldn't hear their words over the barking of the dogs.

"Mr. Hastings won't stand a chance if the shooting starts!" Yocum hissed.

Longarm had it figured that way too. But it had been the rancher's call and just maybe the gang would drop their guns and surrender.

They were out of breath by the time they reached the back of the ranch house. Close now, Longarm could hear the raging argument. He glanced back into the pines and saw that Billy Vail was ready with his Winchester.

"How are we going to handle this?" Yocum asked, voice stretched and thin.

"There's no good way. Let's just walk up behind them. The closer we get the better. And, if they don't panic or get stupid, they ought to see the wisdom in throwing up their hands."

"Gawd, I hope this works!"

"Me too." Longarm stepped out from behind the house with his Colt tight in his fist. He spotted the tall, red-haired Jude Slaney standing next to the buckboard. The Denver executioner was cursing at Ben Hastings who was cussing him right back.

Longarm was just about to yell for the outlaws to freeze, when suddenly, Hastings dragged his shotgun out from under his blanket. The rancher fired point-blank with both barrels at Slaney, flame and smoke belching from his weapon. Slaney took the full blasts directly in the face.

The other outlaws opened fire. Longarm's own gun began to buck in his fist but Hastings was already being riddled in his buckboard. His team of horses bolted and ran as the outlaws turned on Yocum and Longarm.

Up in the trees, Billy Vail's Winchester thundered. Longarm felt the whip-crack of a bullet fly past his ear and he crouched, shooting fast but with accuracy. Two of the cattle rustlers turned to run but Yocum dropped them before they could reach the safety of the ranch house.

And then, almost before it began, the fight was over. The three massive guard dogs threw back their shaggy heads and began to howl.

"Mr. Hastings!" Yocum shouted, racing to the buckboard, which had stopped at the edge of the yard. "Mr. Hastings!"

Longarm knew the old rancher was dead and that he'd died exactly the way he'd wanted.

"Marshal Long! Mr. Hastings is dead!" Yocum yelled, oblivious of the blood seeping down the sleeve of his own shirt.

Longarm counted seven dead J-Bar cowboys, and that didn't include the headless Jude Slaney. Billy hobbled down from the trees and surveyed the carnage.

"Typical Longarm arrest, huh?"

Longarm was in no mood for jokes. "We've got a lot of burying to do before we can go anyplace and I'm the only one fit enough to dig."

"I saw that old man yank out a double-barreled shotgun and blow off Jude's head. He must have known he'd be killed by the others."

"He did," Longarm said. "He went out the way he wanted."

"We should all be that lucky."

"Yeah."

Longarm reloaded his gun and went into the ranch house. He knew he'd find whiskey and he needed a drink.

After that, he'd pack George Avery's body down here and let Billy decide if they should bury Mr. Ludlow's nephew or haul his corpse back to Denver.

"Custis?"

He turned to see Dave Yocum with his badge in his hand. Longarm looked into the young man's eyes and asked, "Dammit, you're not quitting already, are you?"

Yocum surveyed all the dead men, eyes coming to rest on the bloody stump of Jude Slaney's torso. "I just don't think I'm cut out to do this sort of thing, Marshal. I'm real sorry."

"Maybe you'd make a better cattle rancher."

Yocum nodded, eyes moving past Longarm toward the Hastings Ranch. He didn't seem to notice that he'd been wounded and that blood was dripping from his fingertips. "Funny you should mention that because the notion just crossed my mind."

Longarm took the badge and gripped Yocum's thickly calloused but bloody hand. "You'll do just fine. Marry that girl and treat her right."

"Yes, sir."

The muleskinner-about-to-turn-cattle-rancher went to the buckboard and climbed into the seat beside Ben Hastings. Then, without a backward glance, he drove off to find sweet Eloise and help bury her father.

Watch for

LONGARM AND THE WIDOW'S SPITE

276th novel in the exciting LONGARM series
from Jove

Coming in November!

J. R. ROBERTS
THE
GUNSMITH